COSCOM
ENTERTAINMENT

ALSO BY A.P. FUCHS

Blood of My World Trilogy

Discovery of Death
Memories of Death
Life of Death

Undead World Trilogy

Blood of the Dead
Possession of the Dead

THE AXIOM-MAN™ SAGA
(listed in reading order)

Axiom-man
Episode No. 0: First Night Out
Doorway of Darkness
Episode No. 1: The Dead Land
City of Ruin
Of Magic and Men (comic book)

OTHER FICTION

A Stranger Dead
A Red Dark Night
April (writing as Peter Fox)
Magic Man (deluxe chapbook)
The Way of the Fog (The Ark of Light Vol. 1)
Devil's Playground (written with Keith Gouveia)
On Hell's Wings (written with Keith Gouveia)
Zombie Fight Night: Battles of the Dead
Magic Man Plus 15 Tales of Terror
Undeniable

ANTHOLOGIES (as editor)

Dead Science
Elements of the Fantastic
Vicious Verses and Reanimated Rhymes: Zany
Zombie Poetry for the Undead Head

NON-FICTION

Book Marketing for the
Financially-challenged Author

POETRY

The Hand I've Been Dealt
Haunted Melodies and Other Dark Poems
Still About A Girl

Go to
www.canisterx.com
&
www.undeadworldtrilogy.com

Life of Death

A. P. Fuchs

COSCOM ENTERTAINMENT
WINNIPEG

ISBN 978-1-926712-85-7

PUBLISHED BY COSCOM ENTERTAINMENT
www.coscomentertainment.com
Text set in Garamond; Printed and bound in the USA
COVER ART BY C.J. HUTCHINSON

For Belle

Life
of Death

Poisonous

Love is supposed to be pure
Supposed to be sure
But instead, here I am
Poisonous

This isn't a fairytale, or perfection complete
Perfection concrete
But instead, you and me
Poisonous

Why is pain haunting us?
Wanting us
Breaking us
Poisonous

If only we could reach out and lay hold of simpler times
Simply sublime
But instead, this confusion is
Poisonous

Who would have thought it could be
Could be free
But instead, there's a cost
Poisonous

Our love is thick upon us
Consuming us
Making us
Poisonous

1

ROSE STOPPED AT the foot of the cave, mouth open. Zach faced away from her, his head dipped low, crouched over something large and hairy in his arms. The wet slurps and sucking as he devoured the creature in front of him turned Rose's stomach, but at the same time drew her in, as if watching this somehow brought her closer to him.

Zach looked over his shoulder, his face coated in blood, his cheek and forehead bones highly pronounced. With a hiss, he bore his fangs, then got back to work sucking the life out of what Rose now made out as a bear.

It just wandered in here, Zach said in her mind. *I was thirsty. I had to try. Leave me alone.*

She simply nodded even though he couldn't see her, and left the cave and went for a walk not far into the surrounding forest.

It had been two days since they first arrived here, since she first woke up in the cave that, for now, had become their home.

Upon waking up here, Zach brought her into his arms and held her close as he gently told her that while he flew them to safety, he heard his mother bite into Marcus.

"He's dead, Rose," he had said. "I'm sorry."

The sharp searing pain of grief exploded in her heart and the tears burst forth immediately, as images of her father lying there helpless while Mira drank his blood danced before her mind's eye.

She had spent most of that day crying, Zach by her side, letting her work through the pain.

"I'm sorry," he said every few minutes. She knew he meant well, but it quickly got annoying. He'd said he was apologizing so often because it was his mother that drank her father's blood. It was his *kind* that murdered the only family she had left.

She wanted to run, scream, hide, and get away from Zach and let him rot in the cave. And she did—run—into the forest, keeping herself purposely in the bands of light streaming through the leafy canopy overhead. Zach didn't follow, but remained in the cave, calling for her to come back.

She had ran until she was out of breath, and collapsed near the foot of a large oak tree and cried for what seemed like hours. After, spent, hungry, broken, she tried to remember the way back to the cave.

It wasn't Zach's fault her father died. If she really wanted to blame him, she'd say his engaging her father was what led to her dad's death.

I was only trying to do what was best for us, his voice had said inside her mind. *It'll be dark soon and I'll come and get you. Just stay where you are and I'll be there shortly.*

Rose didn't listen, but instead walked with arms crossed back to where she thought the cave was. An hour later, she was still in the forest, weaving around trees and bushes, her heartbeat quickly gaining speed the darker and darker it got. There was barely enough light to see the forest turning gray in the fading daylight. She stood still . . . and waited for Zach. When he came, he gave her fair warning in her mind so he wouldn't startle her. He came up behind her and wrapped her in his arms, took her into the air and flew her back to the cave.

They spent that night in each other's arms, Rose occasionally falling into fits of tears, her dreams peppered with images of her dad's throat being torn out, and waited until morning.

Now, out here in the woods, after watching Zach drink the bear's blood, Rose kept close enough to the cave so she wouldn't get lost again. Her stomach growled from hunger, and she was desperately thirsty. There had to be a stream or a river or something around here that she could get a drink from. Even a small town. She had her bank card so money wasn't a huge issue for the time being. Eventually she'd run out, but probably had enough for a few days' worth of food.

A chill swept through her and the air changed. The scent of rain filled her nostrils.

Great. I'm lost and now I'm going to be wet, she thought and folded her arms. "Hope Zach can find me." *Of course he can. His eyesight's so keen he can practically see through solid objects. Even his hearing . . .* "Can you hear me, Zach?" she said. Louder: "Zach?"

She imagined him still hunched over the bear's carcass, mouth covered in blood and bits of flesh as he drank every last ounce of red fluid from the beast's body. She winced at the image. Even though her dad had shown her all sorts of gory pictures and film to help desensitize her, it was one thing to see blood and guts on a screen, another to see it in real life.

"Hope you hurry up."

She came to an area with a little light. Another sweep of cold air rushed by her, producing goosebumps on her arms. High above, the light tip-tap-tapping as millions of raindrops hit the canopy grew in volume until the rain broke through the leaves and made its way to the forest floor. Each chilly drop hitting her and soaking through her clothes sent a shiver up and down her skin.

"Nice," she said flatly, and started walking back in the direction she'd came. Maybe she'd recognize a knot in a tree or an arrangement of bush and get herself back on track to the cave.

And, Zach, if you can hear me, I could use a lift. You know I never liked the rain, she thought.

"I know," he said.

She looked up with a start. Zach had his arms and legs wrapped around a tree like a cat waiting to pounce.

"You shouldn't run off," he said. His face was back to normal, and was clean except for a light tinge of red still on his pale skin. The bear's blood had soaked through his shirt, though, and bits of its flesh still clung to the fabric.

"I didn't. I got lost."

"I'm sorry if I turned you off back there."

She merely pressed her lips together and carefully tried not to think that, yes, his slaughtering the bear did give her stomach a flip. But she couldn't help it and she knew Zach read her mind because he jumped down from the tree and didn't meet her eyes right away.

"Can we go?" she asked, feeling bad he had come for her early due to the rain.

His eyes met hers and he held out his hand. "Sure."

She took it; already his skin was hot even from the muted daylight. She stepped up to him, setting her feet on top of his. He slowly rose off the ground, moved in between the overhanging tree branches, but kept below the canopy itself. He flew with his back to the canopy, her body braced beneath his, his back stopping most of the rain from hitting her.

Up here, away from the forest floor, Rose wished she could stay suspended between heaven and earth forever, protected in Zach's embrace, the world of chaos and the slaughtering of animals far below no longer part of their lives.

But with Zach, that could never be the case.

Gazing up at him as he kept his eyes forward while he flew, she noticed the skin on his face beginning to blister and burn as the UV light still making its way through the forest's canopy struck him. Every so often he would wince as the pain, it seemed, became too much.

"I'm sorry," she said.

"For what?"

"For hurting you. The sun."

"It's okay. Like I told you a long time ago, it's cloud cover so it's bearable. I'll be fine."

"I know. It's just . . . I'm hurting you now. Hurt you by leaving. I'm sorry."

He simply smiled, gave her a peck on the nose, then set his gaze forward again. "Almost there."

She held onto him tight, though she knew she didn't have to. The way his arms were cradled under her, she could almost completely relax and not have to worry about falling.

She could stay up here in his arms, never to return to the ground again.

Z

INSIDE THE CRYPT at Eagle Park Cemetery, tension hung on the air like the stench of garlic. Mira didn't have to read Rain's mind to know he was not pleased with her, however, despite most of this having been her plan, it seemed he was truly keen on seeing it through to completion anyway.

"It has been two days since he left," Rain said. "He's never been on his own to fend for himself."

"He'll be fine," she said, giving him a knowing glance.

"Zach left for the wrong reasons. And you're to blame for it."

"We are going over this ground again, are we?"

"No. We've already talked about it, but your plan to gently bring Rose into our family fell apart the moment you allowed Zach to confront her father."

"All is not lost, my dear," she said and glided across the floor toward him, her feet not once touching the ground. She sat beside him and put her arm around his shoulder. "Though a soldier, always a child," she said, playing with a lock of his dark hair.

"Don't patronize me. Makes me want to . . . bite you."

"Promise?"

"With the kids in their coffins?"

"No." She took her hand back and folded it with the other one in her lap. "Later, while they're out. We'll hunt out there quickly, then hunt each other in here."

"Hmph. I much prefer the rooftop," he said, his voice quiet.

"So do I, but I do not wish for us to be caught given the circumstance."

"Think it'll cause trouble?"

"Not our lovemaking, but—"

Stone slid against stone and Cassie sat up in her coffin. "Night already?" She rolled over out of the coffin, landed on the floor like a cat landing from a tree, then stood and went over to Wil's coffin and kicked it. "Get up!"

"Cassie," Rain said sternly.

A muffled, "Five more minutes," came from inside her brother's coffin.

"Sorry," Cassie said, stretched—not that she needed it—and in doing so rose to the roof of the crypt and sat upside down on the ceiling. "Any news?"

Mira stood. "Not yet. Hopefully soon."

Zach flew not far from the canopy of trees below, the rain beating on his back, the crash of thunder resounding inside his skull every time one of the angels bowled a strike up above. Though he didn't need it, lightning lit his flight path every minute or two, illuminating the forest and ground beneath.

He rolled over and flew onto his back, opened his mouth to the heavens, and let the rain splash inside and wet his tongue. He was so thirsty he could barely stand it, the darkness that rimmed his vision during a kill now constantly in his peripheral, rage pulsing through him so much he had no choice but to leave Rose alone again.

He'd kill her otherwise, the beast within taking over. He'd bleed her dry.

The bear hadn't satisfied him. He thought it might,

but Mira's statement about it needing to be human blood proved itself to be true. It just couldn't be Rose.

The rain not doing anything to quench his thirst, Zach rolled over midair and continued his flight, dipped down, then circled a lake not far from his and Rose's makeshift camp.

She can't live like that, he thought. *Didn't want to leave her alone. Hope she stays sleeping.* He hadn't wanted to wake her nor tell her where he was going. He saw the way she looked at him when she saw him drinking the bear's blood. Slayer or not, there was fear in her gaze.

Fear of the beast within him that never wandered too far, but if he was being honest with himself, it was he who frightened her.

Her heart had sped up then, not from surprise, but from panic. After she left the cave, he swore he'd never let her catch him kill again, man or beast.

Swooping down where the lake met the tree line, the smell of human blood mixed in with the fishy smell of the water. Like someone hit the dimmer switch on him, the darkness around his vision closed in until he couldn't see. Right after, all went blood red, vigor surging through him so powerfully that apprehensive excitement quickly set in.

The smell of blood drew him to a two-storey, wooden cabin on a rise of land along the lake, trees lining the property.

Voices. Breathing. Six lungs inhaling and exhaling. Three people. One whose slow breaths indicated sleep. Two still awake.

No matter.

The thirst took him.

◆ ◆ ◆

The rain at first had been pleasant to fall asleep to . . . until the thunder sent Rose to her feet, her legs all pins and needles. She lay in the cave, alone and awake, curled up against a small alcove of stone while a tiny fire smoldered in a ring of rocks not far from her. Lightning lit up the cave every minute or so, while thunder blasted off the rocky walls around her, booming in her ears as if she was in the middle of the storm itself. What she wouldn't give for a warm, soft bed right now. Even just to lay in Zach's arms and feel protected.

She missed him.

Where was he?

He didn't say how often he has to feed. Maybe he's trying to find another bear? she thought. "Wish he'd get back here soon."

♦ ♦ ♦

Zach approached the property from the lake, landing on the cabin's rear deck. He didn't make a sound as he walked along the wooden floorboards and to the window that looked into the kitchen. Pressing his ear to the glass, he let the miniscule vibrations from the voices within give him a clear picture as to precisely where in the cabin everyone was. The two grownups—male and female— were off to the left in what he presumed was the living room. The other—a child—was down the hallway on the right, sleeping.

Just the adults, he thought. The thirst made his throat ache for the sweet moisture of warm blood, his body yelling out for the awesome strength and euphoria tonight's feeding would bring.

The cabin door was to his left and would open up into a small nook of what was most likely a mudroom before connecting to a hallway that led from the kitchen to the living room.

Go in, go in, go in, he thought. "No," he whispered, "keep it simple. Keep it quick." A low growl rumbled in his throat.

He moved to check his reflection in the kitchen window, but even in the dim moonlight, he couldn't see his human form.

Mother didn't tell me about having no reflection, he thought. *Stay focused. Don't change. Control. Stay in control.*

Zach walked up to the door and knocked on it. His hypersensitive ears picked up a male voice within: "Wait. I think someone knocked." The man shushed the woman beside him.

Zach knocked again.

The man said, "Stay here. I'll see who it is." Footsteps followed, walked past the door, past where Zach stood, the sound of feet on tile now in the kitchen. Out of his peripheral, he caught the man taking a peek at their visitor through the kitchen window. The vampire made a conscious effort to keep a relaxed expression, something friendly.

The footsteps resumed, heavy, and drew nearer as the man inside made his way to the door. The *clicking-clack* of a latch and deadbolt being undone made Zach brim with anticipation.

Soon.

The door opened. The man stood there behind the screen door. "Yeah?"

"Hi," Zach said. "Know what street this is? I was out for a walk and got a little turned around. Trying to find Keller Street. Know which way?" The street name was made up.

"Keller?"

"Yeah, Keller. I think it's east, but I could be wrong. Do you know, or do you got a map?"

The man furrowed his brow as he mulled it over. He called back into the house, "Honey, there isn't a Keller street around here, is there?"

"Who is it?"

"Just a guy out for a walk."

"What? Can't hear you."

The man pinched his lips together and raised his index finger in a gesture to wait. To Zach, "Just—hang on." The man left from behind the screen door and went further into the house.

As Zach heard the guy say, "Some kid at the door. Looking for Keller Street. Not sure where . . ." he let the bones slide beneath his skin and the fangs cut and grow through his gums. His fingers tensed as long, thick nails extended from their tips, sharp and hard.

All was red.

He raised his hand and swiped at the screen door, his razor sharp claws cutting through the mesh and giving him entrance. He jumped into the mudroom just as the man came running. Zach jumped on him immediately, both hands coming down across the man in an X, slashing through the man's face and chest. The man stopped cold, eyes wide with shock, blood spurting from the wounds. Zach licked his fingers, kicked the man to the ground, then used the man's chest as a springboard to pounce on the woman who came running from the living room. With a twist, he rolled her to the ground, used the claw of his index finger to puncture a hole in her neck, then bent down and drank from the wound like a water fountain.

The sweet soothing warmth of blood filled his mouth. He gulped it down, seemingly unable to quench his thirst. The more blood he drank, the more blood he needed.

"Sogoodsogoodsogood . . ." he whispered as the deep red liquid splashed against his lips. He leaned into her further and clamped his mouth around her neck to form a seal, not letting a single drop go to waste.

The blood splashed against his parched insides, bringing back to life the dead man within.

So amazing. So, so good! The euphoria took him as emotions unexpectedly surfaced; a violent collision of joy, hate, sadness, frustration and lust plowed through him like a bulldozer out of control. His body shook from the insane pleasure racking his body, every muscle tensing then relaxing, tensing then relaxing . . .

The man.

Zach jumped from the woman's body and landed on top of the man's chest, facing him. The fellow was still alive, choking on his own blood. The crimson juice bubbled from the man's lips. Zach got close and shoved his palm under the man's chin, snapping his mouth shut, then immediately dove into the tender flesh of the neck. The man's body jerked, twisted once, then moved no more.

As he drank the man's blood, letting it splash on him, envisioning every crimson droplet running down his throat, imagining those that got on him being absorbed by his skin, his ears perked up to the sound of faint, shallow breathing. He slurped in another mouthful of blood, then looked up to see a little girl of no more than four standing there in one-piece jammies—white and dotted with tiny red roses—staring at him. Her blue eyes beneath heavy bangs of dirty blonde hair bore nothing but confusion.

Breathing heavy, still taken by the sheer pleasure of drinking another's blood, Zach merely stared at her, unable to decide if he should say anything or simply act on the impulse to tear her apart and drink her blood, too.

The little girl looked down at her mother's bloody corpse, her large eyes twitching once before tears glazed over them. She looked at Zach, then down at her father's face. Pouting her lips, she looked back at Zach, then down at the smears of blood on the floor.

The darkness swirled around Zach's vision, and the man's blood called to him to finish taking his fill. But this girl . . . she was still alive, still fresh. Her heart beat rapidly in her chest; Zach imagined its panicked energy forcing the blood out of broken veins into his mouth and into his stomach.

The girl began to cry, tears running down her cheeks. It was clear every effort was made to not cry out loud, maybe because she was in the presence of a stranger.

Don't, he told himself. An image of Rose flashed before his eyes. The little girl came into focus again. She was like Rose, in a way, an only child. Her parents were taken from her, like Rose's. *Don't. Don't.*

Zach stood, his legs wobbly beneath him, the joy of fresh blood making its way through his system causing him to be light-headed.

The girl took a step back.

Zach imagined reaching out for her, picking up her tiny body, and clamping his fangs around her neck. The girl's body locked in his arms when he pierced her and the blood began to flow. The more he drank, the limper she got until, eventually, she slumped in his arms altogether. He was proud of her for not screaming, for not even crying. Such bravery.

Zach expected the fantasy to flee from before his mind's eye, but instead, he sat on the ground, covered in blood, with the girl in his arms, and realized it hadn't been a fantasy at all.

H

The cave was chilly; the fire had burned down long ago. Rose shivered in the dark, kneeling before the warm embers that remained of a once-brilliant fire. There was just enough warmth to soothe her hands and forearms.

Sleep really hadn't been an option. She had dozed a little bit, but being here alone in the cave was not conducive to lasting comfort.

She thought of her father and mother, images of their faces flickering before her eyes in a barrage of painful memories. So removed from society, her life, everything she knew—what she wouldn't give for a chance to see her father again, to ask him why all this happened. The man he was—*truly* was—she had only just been getting to know. The new man was someone she was falling in love with, like having two fathers for the price of one.

"Hope God lets you come back, Dad," she said. "Even if I couldn't see you, just to know you're there, still allowed to be a soldier and finish what you started." She sighed. "But you did finish, I guess. You . . . passed away. Just hope and wish you feel a sense of accomplishment now, a sense of completion." She smirked. "They say ghosts stay behind because the dead have unfinished business. Wonder if you'll come back because you feel the same way."

She clenched her teeth and swallowed the pain and heartache that built in her chest.

A cool hand touched her shoulder; she jumped up with a yelp.

"I'm sorry," Zach said from somewhere in the dark.

"I didn't hear you."

"I'm sorry."

"You need to tell me you're there. Especially when I can't see anything."

"It's going to be light soon. Did you get any rest?"

"No." Then, "Why did you leave?"

"I was . . . thirsty. I had to."

"What about the bear?"

"It wasn't enough. It wasn't anything. I'm sorry you saw me like that."

I hope I never have to again, she thought.

"You won't," he said.

"Not now, Zach. Leave my mind alone."

"If that's your wish."

"It is."

"Then I will respect that."

There was silence between the two of them. Rose knew she was being grouchy from lack of sleep. Hopefully she'd be able to rest soon—Zach, too—and later this afternoon they could figure out their next move.

"I'm going to lie down," she said. "Anything special you need to do to rest because, well, you know?"

"No. I will be fine. Do you want me near you?"

Her body ached for him, but her mind said otherwise. She just wasn't sure what he was like when he slept and if she would be safe. But to ask him that . . . it was too embarrassing. "I'll be okay," she said. "Nothing personal."

"As you wish."

She put out her hand to locate the cave wall and find a spot next to it so she could lie down. Instead of rock, her hand met cloth and flesh. Zach's shirt was wet and she didn't need to see it to know it was blood.

"Gross," she said and shook her hand out.

"Rose?"

"Yes?"

"Do I scare you?"

She sighed. "In a way, but not in a *bad* way, if that makes sense. I'm not scared of you directly, just everything changing so quickly for both of us and the fear of possibly not getting used to you or your world." *I hope you understand.* She waited a moment, anticipating him to respond to her thoughts. Zach remained quiet.

"I'm happy I don't scare you," he said quietly, then added, "like that. Never thought this would happen for either of us. Who could?"

Never thought . . . "You remember before? All of it?"

"Not all, but more and more each day as I'm with you. Thanks for that. Makes *us* all the deeper."

She understood because she felt the same way about him. Having two histories—pre-undead and post-undead—added an extra dimension to their relationship others rarely, if ever, had.

Rose held out her hand, this time hoping for his fingers to touch hers. When they did, she let him pull her close. In the dark, his fingers ran through her hair, down her neck, around her shoulders and down to her waist. His electric touch removed any fear of tonight's shadows from her.

"Come with me," he said, and scooped her up in his arms.

Exhilaration swept through her as he took her out of the dark of the cave and into the pre-morning sky, one that was now clear of rain, had only a few remaining clouds, and was bathed a bright purple.

She looked at Zach, the touch of rouge on his cheeks and around his mouth now not as disturbing as she thought it'd be. This was just who he was. He couldn't help it. She could love him anyway. Right?

The vampire took her over the trees, the cool predawn air refreshing against her skin after spending so much time in the cave.

Soon, a lake appeared below them and Zach flew them across it, just above the water. Rose's wavering reflection stared back at her. She marveled at it, only able to see her body flying above the water, Zach's reflection absent.

"Can you . . . hold me so I can fly lying down like you?" she asked, feeling a little silly for asking it.

He smiled. "Sure." And adjusted her so he was on top, holding her from behind, her face and body now parallel with the lake.

A smiling girl looked back at her from the water's surface, one with her arms out and spirit free. One that seemed suddenly unburdened despite the stress of the last few days.

One day I want to fly, she thought.

Her body elevated from the lake and Zach adjusted his hold on her once again so she was back in his arms. He slowly lowered them down on a wooden dock, one that led up to a cabin on a small hill.

"While I was away tonight," he said, "I found this place. We can stay here. We'll be safe."

Safe? What about— "Are you sure?"

"No one's there."

"Isn't that trespassing?"

"It's only temporary."

A lump settled in her stomach. It didn't feel right. What about the people who owned this place? What if they came here and found them?

"I don't think I can," she said.

"I've already checked inside."

"You did?"

"Mm-hm. There's a calendar in there, days marked off. No one's going to be here for over two months."

Yawning, she took a few steps down the dock, hands on her hips. "I don't know," she said and turned around to face him.

Zach's face and hands were beginning to blister, the sky behind him melting from purple to orange.

It was almost dawn.

ROUND 11 A.M. Rose awoke, the heavy weight of sadness sitting on her chest like an invisible anvil. The bed was warm, covered in a down quilt, pillows stacked two high. By the time she and Zach arrived at the cabin, she was so exhausted that falling asleep in a stranger's bed hadn't caused her much distress.

She rolled over from her back onto her side and gazed at the closet with the dual-mirror sliding door. Zach was inside there, away and out of the daylight that still found its way into the bedroom through the cracks in the blinds. She hoped he was sleeping. She wished she could get back to sleep, too.

Rose closed her eyes and let the fatigue swimming around her head suck her back into the dark place of sleep, with hopefully good dreams to come. Instead, the heartache of losing her father once more set its firm hand upon her, longing for him building up until she couldn't take it anymore and quietly got out of bed. The hallway that ran outside the room had an old maroon carpet, flat and worn from a couple decades of walking. The strong scent of disinfectant hung on the air.

"Weird," she said.

The emptiness of the cabin seemed to make itself apparent by creating the sense that each room was larger than it was, each somehow monitored by the family that owned it and that they, wherever they were, were able to see her making her way to the living room through camera surveillance.

The living room was simply laid out: a couch and loveseat to one side of the room, situated in an L-shape; the TV entertainment unit across from the couches, the TV on, remote on the coffee table in front of the couch.

Yawning, Rose went to the old white couch, the pink flowers that dotted the fabric not interesting her all that much, then sat down and picked the remote off the coffee table. She put her feet up on the couch cushions beside her and began thumbing through the channels. Some daytime talk shows, an infomercial, a truck commercial, something with a guy eating bugs—not much on.

"There's, like, a dozen channels," she said to the remote. "Nothing—Wait." She searched her memory of coming here as the sun began its ascent into the sky, trying to recall if the television had been on when they first arrived. Between the extreme fatigue from hardly sleeping plus the early morning light coming in through the windows, she wasn't sure if she noticed and didn't recall *hearing* anything either. Unless the television had been on mute. Did Zach watch TV?

No, he couldn't, she thought, *not this morning anyway. This room is too bright. He wouldn't survive.*

She sat there, staring at the TV but not really watching, its images just something to set her eyes on. So many things ran through her mind, some of which of what to do with her father's death when she returned to the city, who to tell, how to end her parents' real estate business or how to sell it, school, the house—everything. She reached up to her cheeks and brushed away the tears, not remembering them spilling out.

Her and Zach couldn't stay here. They needed a plan, but what could one do when your world was life and another's was death?

◆ ◆ ◆

"I want the word spread tonight," Mira said that evening. To Wil and Cassie, "Children, tonight when you roam the streets, those of our kind must know that Zach is required to return here immediately. I want everyone looking for him."

"Won't that make you look incompetent, Mother?" Cassie asked.

Mira shot her a sharp look. "No, because the rest of the community does not know Zach, or even of him. I've kept his turning a secret until now."

"And if we find him?" Wil asked.

"Draw him here as peacefully as possible," she said. "Only take him by force if necessary. Once he comes—regardless of how he comes—that girl will be sure to follow, and she will be our portal to the inner workings of the slayers."

"We should turn her once we extract what we want to know," Rain said.

"Perhaps," Mira said. She then came over to him and sat on his lap. With both hands around his neck, she added, "If the storm clears. She might turn and not remember anything. At present, all information is valuable."

"Of course, my love," he said and pecked her on the nose.

She gripped his face in her hands and pressed her mouth against his, the coolness of his dead tongue sending shivers of excitement for intimate times later on throughout her body.

We must find him, she projected to the others. *Find your brother, find our son.*

◆ ◆ ◆

In the dark of the closet, Zach lay with his hands folded across his chest, body perfectly still, mouth slightly open. He was awake, his tongue already tasting the night's feed. Rose was not in the bedroom, he knew, and could hear her heart beating in the living room. Her breathing was slow, which meant she was asleep.

There are more around here, he thought, thinking of the other cabins rimming the lake. When he flew by them the other day, heartbeats echoed from a few of the cabins whereas others remained silent. The main issue would be pacing. If he visited one cabin per night, he had maybe enough blood to last him a couple of weeks, three if he stretched it. The problem was each cabin held more than one person, so if one was to be fed upon, they all had to be. Unless . . .

I can draw them out one at a time, take them into the woods. "But that wouldn't work," he whispered. "They'd become a missing person. It would draw attention." *It could become a feast.* "Or it would spell your end, especially if a new group of slayers got word of the disappearances."

No, he would have to kill like he had those that occupied this house. He and Rose would have to be on the move soon.

Zach rolled over onto his side and peeked through the crack under the closet. The room beyond was pitch black, which meant the sun had already set. Good.

He rose to his feet, bent at the waist, the top of his back brushing against the clothes hanging in the closet. He opened the closet doors and stepped out.

The hallway was dark as well. Rose was on the couch, half sitting, half laying, the TV on across from her, the sound mute.

The moment he laid eyes on her, his concern for the night's feeding began to melt away. Eyes closed, breathing steady, lips together and slightly curled up in a small smile, Rose was the pinnacle of beauty. A sleeping beauty. Even now as he stood over her, his body ached to hover above her sleeping form, gently lower himself onto her and just hold her, kiss her head, her cheeks, her neck.

He placed a hand on her shoulder. "Rose?" he said softly.

She stirred, the slight smile on her face vanishing, then reappearing again when she slipped back off into sleep.

What if . . . Zach knelt down beside her and leaned close, his head not far from hers. He focused on her mind, the image of raindrops splashing against the puddles of thought inside her head, the shape of each splash and the way the liquid rippled outward as a result—and stepped into her mind.

Rose dreamed in a picture frame, whatever she saw rimmed by a red and black outline, one that was fluid and moved like a square of liquid.

She sat in a mall, one that looked familiar though Zach couldn't remember the name of it. People milled about, their clothing and faces smudged so it was difficult to make out exact details. Rose sat at a table in the center of the mall, a glass-encased elevator to her right, the second tier of the mall above her and on either side, a golden banister rimming the upper level.

At the table, Rose had a glass of water on one side of it, a glass of chocolate bars on the other. Voices were on the air, a cacophony of several hundred people talking at once. Even with his ultra-sensitive hearing, Zach couldn't distinguish the words. Not here. Not in this world of dream.

Rose got up from the table, took the glass of chocolate bars with her, and handed it off to an elderly lady passing by. Rose said to her, "Don't use purple elastics when you eat these. They'll stick to your dentures and you'll have to get them replaced."

The elevator came down just as Rose approached it. A handful of blurry-faced people in black clothing stepped off the elevator and she got on.

Zach zipped toward her in a burst of speed and got in the elevator just before the door closed. He glanced down at his body. There was none. He was merely a set of eyes peering through the looking glass into Rose's world.

"I'm happy you came," Rose said, still facing the doors.

"You can see me?" Zach said, or at least he thought she did. Rose didn't respond, as if she didn't hear him.

The elevator started to rise to the second level.

Rose turned toward him; a figure came up behind her, materializing in the elevator. As it came into focus, Zach saw it was himself. The vampire put his hands around Rose from behind, opened his mouth to bear his fangs, the rest of his features still smooth, and brushed his teeth gently across her neck. Rose closed her eyes and seemed to enjoy it.

He didn't transform, Zach thought. Perhaps a normal visage with sharp fangs was how Rose preferred to see him, or simply how her mind projected him here in this dream world.

She closed her eyes, letting herself go in his embrace. The vampire kissed her neck, ran his hands down to her hips, then slowly brought them back up and caressed her shoulders, her arms.

"Rose," Zach said, reaching out to her and slightly wondering if the vampire in this dream could sense him, if the undead across the way was linked to him somehow.

The idea of a mental connection was all it took, and Zach was sucked across the elevator, past Rose's body, and into the vampire beyond. What was once before the absence of touch suddenly transformed into full sensation as his hands felt her arms beneath his palms, his lips upon her neck, the scent of her skin.

My counterpart and I . . . merged. He could only suppose his ability to enter and read minds went beyond mere observance and could become something deeper should he choose, an avatar among the other virtual beings that inhabited a person's dreams.

He paused his caress, his kiss, listening inside himself for any sign of the dream version of him to say or think something. All was quiet.

Could she control me because this shell I wear is part of her mind? Or will she let what happens happen and it's that simple? It didn't matter, he decided.

"Rose," he said softly.

"Mm?" she said, the little lilt she put at the end of her inquiry a reminder of one of the many reasons why he loved her in the first place.

Gently, he turned her around, just as the elevator doors opened on the second level.

"This is our floor," she said, almost as if forgetting they had just been in an intimate embrace.

"It is?"

Rose glanced out the elevator doors. Faceless people came up to the doors but did not enter. Many just came, looked inside for a moment, then turned and went on their way.

"It's too crowded out there," she said. With her index finger, she poked at the silver circular buttons next to the door on the right. They weren't numbered.

Zach thought it best to just play along and see where her dreamscape took him. "Where to, then?"

Rose eyed the silver circles and ran her index finger over them as she decided on her selection. She settled on the bottom right button and pressed it. The elevator doors closed.

"Where are we going?" Zach asked.

"Downstairs," was all she said.

5

THE DOORS OPENED and instead of revealing a basement hallway or a storage room as expected, they opened to a department store, the kitchenwares section just ahead of them. Rose stepped out and Zach followed. She took his hand and led him around the aisles of cookware, past the tables of knife blocks, microwaves, non-stick pots and pans and to the housewares section.

At the end of the first aisle was a short bed showcasing a gray-and-white-patched quilt, matching pillowcases around plush and poofy pillows. Zach noticed what was supposed to be a sale sign instead contained symbols he couldn't read. He briefly recalled something from his past life about how reading in one's dreams wasn't easy and usually required tremendous focus.

Rose sat at the edge of the bed and patted the spot next to her. He sat down. The scene changed and instead of sitting, they both lay on the bed, side by side, facing each other, their noses almost touching.

"I thought you were sleeping," Rose said.

"We just laid down," he replied.

"I was sleeping, having a good dream."

"About me?"

"About flying through the sky, faster than a speeding bullet."

"Was I there?"

"Just me. I loved it. It was awesome." She glanced up at his forehead then back down to his face. "Why did we wake up?"

"Rose, we've been awake this whole time. You're not making any sense."

"Don't talk to me like that. I always make sense. Let's sleep again."

He only assumed her confusion was because this was a dream and not everything was clear. "Okay."

She closed her eyes. The scene shifted again: they were still on the bed, but Rose was on top of him. He couldn't feel the weight of her body. Was he just a spectator again? He was still inhabiting his dream counterpart. He supposed sensation was spotty in dreams and not everything was felt.

"Can I give you a kiss?" she asked, eyes now open and wide with anticipation.

"Yes. Please."

Gently, she leaned close and pressed her lips against his. He felt her face sink into him as she lightly licked the tip of his tongue, moved her lips around his own, her breath warming the interior of his mouth.

He ran his hands down her back, caressing her and drawing her closer, as close as possible.

Her lips left his as she moved and kissed his cheek, then his jawline and neck.

"You mean everything to me," she said. "I missed you so so much." She pulled away. "Be with me."

"I am. Always."

"No," she said and brought his hand to her face, using it to cup her cheek. "Be with me. I want to make love to you."

This isn't real, Rose, he thought. *That kind of thing . . .* Well, he supposed it *was* possible. They had just kissed after all. A memory surfaced, and he remembered before his rebirth they had promised not to be intimate, not until they were older or even married. *Would mean more that way,*

Rose had said at the time. And he agreed. He still did despite wanting so desperately for them to come together, explore each other's bodies, to become one and revel in the pleasure they could give each other both physically and emotionally.

But . . . it's a dream, he thought. *It wouldn't really happen, if we did. Nothing here is real.* Except for knowing that he betrayed her wishes, he knew. It was something he couldn't bring himself to bear.

"Oh Rose," he whispered. "I love you with my whole heart. Truly. How about something different, maybe even better?"

She furrowed her brow, trying to figure out what he meant.

With a soft smile, he held her tight, floated up off the quilt, rolled them over so she was on the bottom, then laid her down gently.

"Kiss me," she said.

"Not yet." He gazed into her eyes, past them, envisioning her thoughts as tangible objects beyond, little flutters of light against a background of blood.

This was the first time he had entered a dream, and now he was going to enter—not another, but her mind, her heart.

Zach focused on the flits of light, pushed his mind into hers, mentally grabbing hold of the wisps of soft light as they danced in a swirling ballet. Entwined and wound—he let himself get swept up with them until he felt he was connected enough to take control.

All flashed black for a moment, and when the black dispersed, he saw he was in Rose's body, in her dream, on the bed, his vampire dream counterpart above him, not moving.

I'm inside her, he thought. *I'm in—*

"I can hear you, Zach," she said, her body in the dream able to move, his mind inside, a part of her yet still separate.

Amazing, he thought.

"It is. Where are you?"

Inside you.

"Where?"

Your mind.

"Really?"

Yes.

"What are you going to do, I thought we were going to—"

Lay still. I'll do the rest. He wasn't sure what he meant by that. It seemed the world of the dream had infiltrated him as well, dictating words and actions like a puppeteer pulling strings.

He felt his body inside her body, as if she was an outfit of silk. The inside of her skin held no temperature other than something neutral, just enough to let him know he wore her.

The flits of light of Rose's thoughts—perhaps even consciousness—surrounded his vision. From within her body, he reached out and grabbed hold of them, treating them with the utmost care. He ran his hands along their length, his touch and theirs meeting with a spark.

Rose cooed.

Zach kissed the light.

Rose shivered.

He brought it close, caressed it, stroked it, wrapped himself in it.

She writhed on the bed from the pleasurable tingles each stroke of the light bore upon her.

Zach's body moved with hers, too, temporarily feeling the same pleasure before finding himself back entwined with the light.

"More . . ." she purred.

Zach took the light, stroked his hands around it, applying more pressure in some places and less in others.

Rose moaned from each touch; giggled a couple times.

He kissed the light, caressed it, told it he loved it.

I want to be with you forever.

"I want to be with you, too," she said.

Stay with me always.

"I will."

Promise.

"I do."

Zach twirled the sheet of light and wrapped it around himself like a cloak, moving, floating and twisting as he rubbed it all over his body.

Rose's breathing grew heavier, her breaths getting progressively shorter.

With a surge of energy, Zach flew the cloak of light around this strange place of blood red, bouncing himself off the other bands of light that flickered here. Every time he struck a spark of light, Rose moaned. He flew faster, rubbing against each spark, lingering on some, just brushing past others.

Her breaths grew even shorter apart. Her moans rose in volume.

With a twirl, Zach grabbed another band of light, brought it inside the cloak with him, kissed it, held it, stroked it, and hoped that somehow Rose could feel his heart.

She breathed deeper, moaned louder.

Zach spun around the other sparks, moving between each of them as fast as he could, every touch against them electricity to his own skin.

Rose moaned and the entire world of light vibrated as

if in an earthquake, the sparks exploding in shimmering rays of brilliant white and yellow.

The cloak of light around Zach began to dim and he fell into the endless abyss of red, further and further until he pulled himself out of her mind, and was above her again on the bed.

He kissed her neck, held her close, and brushed his lips against hers.

"I love you," he said.

"I love you, too," she breathed, her eyes slightly damp.

They held each other, Rose quivering in his arms. Soon, she began to dissolve and the department store around them began to do the same.

As much as he wanted to be here with her, Zach said good-bye. Rose's face was blank, as if she wasn't sure what he meant.

He pulled himself out of her mind, and was back kneeling before her by the couch just as she awoke. When she saw him, she smiled and sat up enough to get her arms around him and squeeze him tight.

6

MIRA STOOD OUTSIDE the family mausoleum. It was a little after eleven at night and the cemetery had been closed since nine. Her family stood behind her, even her husband for he knew this was her doing, her plan.

All was in motion now, with the undead dispatched throughout the city and the province to bring Zach home and, with him, Rose.

"She is the key to all this," Mira said.

"I retrieved from Zach's mind that she, too, is a slayer like her father was," Rain said.

"Indeed. She will be easy to break once we have her."

"Most likely she has received training to avoid telepathic intrusion."

"She is a novice. Infiltrating her mind and extracting the information we need will not be difficult."

"How can you be so sure?"

"You forget your place, Rain," she said firmly.

He came up beside her and slightly dipped at the waist. "You are right, my love. It is not my place to question you. However, why not bite her, drink, and extract the memories from her blood?"

"As you know, not all of the life taken is shared. What will be revealed might not be what we want to see. We cannot take that risk. I know what I am doing."

"Once more, you have my apologies."

"Are you going to hurt him, Mother?" Cassie asked.

"Your father? No, of course not."

"I meant Zach."

She turned, lips tautly pursed. She did not like to be made a fool of, especially right after reminding someone to beware what they say. "He will not be harmed so long as he cooperates."

"Why wouldn't he?" Wil asked.

Mira shot him an icy stare. "Do I need to repeat myself? I certainly hope not."

Wil just looked at her, mouth slightly agape. As fond of him as she was, he wasn't the sharpest fang in the set. "Your brother has been compromised, corrupted, and is swayed he can coexist with a human."

"If he wasn't so in love with her, he would be the perfect one to extract the info we need," Rain said.

"His love for her will be his undoing if he's not careful," Mira said. "Should Rose carry the secrets we desire, it will not be long until the slayer order falls and our kind will be able to roam the world freely and, person by person, transform it into a utopia for our race. Humanity will be but an echo among the halls of history, if we succeed."

◆ ◆ ◆

The Flin Flon bar's parking lot was full for the night, the folks within drinking up and hooking up in an effort to right the boredom of living in a small town.

Zach stood across the road from the bar, watching and waiting for another round of smokers to exit and step outside for a puff.

Rose was back at the cabin. He told her he wouldn't be long and he hoped indeed that would be the case. He missed her already, the sensation of longing for her something he wasn't used to, but ever since intertwining himself with her dream, his perception of her and all of reality had changed and he was able to truly *feel* for the first time since his rebirth.

Across the way, the doors to the bar opened and a group of two guys and one girl, all appearing under the age of twenty, came out. They all wore jeans, each with a light jacket. After pulling packs of cigarettes and lighters from their pockets and lighting up, the girl laughed, the pitch of her voice so high it pierced Zach's sensitive ears.

"As if," the girl said.

"Hey, you started it," said one of the guys, this one with dirty blond hair hanging partly over his eyes.

"I so did not text him," she said.

"Whatever. The guy's now all excited, thinks you like him, and all that."

"Ooooh, smoochies," said another guy. Head shaved, Zach could see the veins pulsate under the veneer. An image of cracking open the skull like a melon and letting a geyser of crimson rain gush upon him flashed. Intrigued with the idea, the beast within scratched at the walls he had desperately tried to build.

"What are you, in high school again?" she asked.

Shaved Head said, "Look who's talking, getting all upset over a text." In a high-pitched, girly voice he added, "Oh, gee, I hope he doesn't think I like him. Oh no. What if he thinks I do and I have to go out with him?"

"Shut up!" she said, and took a drag off her cigarette.

Zach rushed in. "I don't think it'll be that big a deal."

The first guy, the one with dirty blond hair, said, "What's it to you?"

Zach shrugged. "Nothing. Just couldn't help but overhear."

Shaved Head said, "Where'd this guy come from? Yo, you better beat it, man."

Meeting her eyes, Zach asked the girl, "Have you ever

seen Italy?" He maintained eye contact even when Shaved Head told him to bug off.

The girl chuckled. "No, why?"

Slowly, Zach raised his hand. "I can take you there, if you let me." *Come to me,* he told her.

Her eyes went glossy and she started toward him.

"Karen, where you going?" Dirty Blond asked.

She didn't reply, but instead took Zach's hand. Shaved Head stepped in and separated their fingers. He then came up to Zach, nose-to-nose, and puffed out his chest. "Beat it before I beat you."

To the girl: *Come to me.*

"Steve, I want to go with him," Karen said from behind him.

Steve furrowed his brow.

Come to me.

Karen shoved in between Zach and Steve. "Please," she said, "don't do this. I'll go with him."

"Like hell you will."

Come to me.

Taking his hand in hers, she told Zach, "Let's go."

"Very well," Zach said, his eyes never leaving Steve's. The other guy just stood in the back, chuckling to himself and sucking on his smoke.

Putting his arm around her, Zach turned Karen away from her friends. After taking no more than three steps, Steve grabbed Zach by the shoulder. Bone shuffled against bone, muscles stretched, teeth and nails elongated—and Zach spun around, jumped on Steve and bit into his neck, ripping out his jugular.

Karen, still entranced, merely looked on.

The other guy swore and made a break for the bar door.

Zach was there in an instant and swept in between

the guy and door. Swiftly, he slashed open the guy's neck in one quick motion, grabbed him by the throat, blood running over his hands, and took a large gulp of the sweet red nectar gushing from the guy's neck.

With a growl, he dropped the body, sped to Karen, and took her in his arms.

She didn't say anything, merely looked down at her friends' bodies as she and Zach drifted into the air, without shedding even a tear.

High in the sky, well out of range from anyone below looking upward, Zach opened his mouth wide and with a quick jerk yanked Karen's head toward him. His teeth clamped down on her neck. Her body went rigid from the pain and then slowly relaxed as the blood was drained from her body. The sweet crimson liquid that pumped through her veins reached deep into Zach's soul and filled his body with the glorious pleasure of drinking her blood.

Come to me, he whispered into her mind.

Even though he held her close, she weakly took hold of him and tried to draw herself even closer, embed her neck even more into his fangs, letting him drink the life away from her.

The warmth of blood went down Zach's throat, leaked from his lips, ran down his neck and shirt.

The moment Karen's heart stopped, Zach let her go, growled, then dropped her body. He heard the air whistle around it as it plummeted to the bar's parking lot below to join her friends' corpses. A moment more and the heavy splat of flesh and bone slamming into the pavement found its way to his ears.

Rejuvenated, he waited as the girl's memories went through him, then turned to the right midair and flew back to Rose.

He didn't want to keep her waiting.

7

LATE NIGHT TELEVISION has got to be the worst invention known to man, Rose thought as she flipped through the channels. Aside from a couple of infomercials, the weather station, and a couple of shows she never heard of, there wasn't anything on. Not that she expected there to be anything substantial on this late anyway, but she had hoped for a repeat of *The Tonight Show* or something she recognized.

She had the cabin to herself, Zach out there doing what he needed to do to stay alive.

The sick part is, she thought, *I'm starting to get used to it. Even starting to accept it.* "Rose Jordan, accomplice to murder," she whispered. Sure, she wasn't out there with him helping him obtain his victims, but she *knew* that's what he was doing and in the eyes of the law, knowing was enough. It was her duty to report it.

"As if they would believe me," she said. "Oh yes, hi, I'd like to report a vampire. Uh-huh. Yes, I'm telling the truth. Yes, sir, he's out there right now biting into people's throats so he can stay alive." She rolled her eyes. *Dad held back from showing me everything because he took care of it himself. I still need more time. What's become of me?* Her duty was to stop the vampire threat, not become a part of it. Even though he was dead, she sensed her father looking on, arms crossed, eyes boring into her, wanting her to finish what she and him started not long ago.

"I can do it, Dad," she said. "I just need time to sort things out. If it wasn't for Zach, I could do it, but I've seen the side of them that you didn't see. I was in their home and I was fine. I was actually *welcomed.*" She exhaled slowly. "I had a family again."

She turned the TV off and just sat on the couch in the dim lighting from the single lamp in the living room. A few minutes later, sick of the silence, she said, "I need some air."

Rose got up, went to the door and got out onto the steps. The air was cool, clean, the trees surrounding the property a series of shadows watching over her, the lake a shiny matt reflecting the stars and moon above.

A foul smell hit her nostrils, one of burnt rubber and sweaty socks. She put her finger under her nose to block it.

Nice. Come outside to breathe and a stupid skunk comes along and farts. "Yuck."

She went down the steps and headed toward the dock, away from the cabin, hoping to get out of the smell's range.

The further she went down the path leading to the dock, the freer she felt from the weight of the cabin, the haunting thoughts of her part in Zach's murders, and the harsh smell of skunk spray.

Her feet clunked against the dock's wooden boards accompanied by the sloshing sound of small waves splashing up against the dock beneath her feet. She took a deep breath through her nose, getting a lungful of the lake's air.

The water splashed against the dock again, its rhythm a pleasant distraction from the silence all around.

Too much quiet and, ironically, you can't think.

The water sloshed against the dock. Rose stepped up to the edge and gazed down into the dark, murky water of the lake.

She leaped back with a yelp when a face stared back at her from just beneath the water's surface.

"Oh no," she breathed and put her hands to her mouth. Cautiously, she peered over the edge again.

A small body lay beneath the water's surface, the peaceful face of a little girl with her eyes closed, half floating, the side of her neck torn out in milky ribbons of flesh and skin.

Tears immediately wet Rose's eyes. She looked away, and stepped up to the other side of the dock. And there, slightly beneath the water's surface on that side, were two more bodies, a man and a woman's, both like the girls: arched slightly back, half floating in the lake. Like the girl's, their necks had been ripped open, and the man's face was a mix of pink and white, like a tea towel that had been shredded and laid on top of a skull.

Rose glanced back at the cabin, then back to the bodies in the water.

Zach had lied to her.

◆ ◆ ◆

Cassie let her mind spread over the air like a satellite searching for a frequency. Her brother was out there and if she was fortunate, following the thoughts of both human and vampire alike would eventually lead her to him.

Wil flew beside her, mouth shiny and red from a light snack before they left.

She honed in on any thoughts that indicated a sense of fear. Thousands of words in various voices in a multitude of languages filled her mind, saturated her brain and pulled her in numerous directions.

"Needle in a haystack," she said.

"Don't worry," Wil said. "I'm searching, too."

"I think it'd be best if we split up."

"Agreed. Shall we hone in on the large areas and avoid the small?"

She knew he was referring to mental indicators where fearful and panicked thoughts seemed to congregate over a larger area as opposed to isolated incidents peppered throughout the city streets. "Yes," she said, "and use our kin as beacons in those areas."

"Done. Be in touch."

"Likewise."

Wil banked off to the right and went his own way.

Cassie listened to the restless and frightful calls of the humans below, keeping a mental ear open for anything that would indicate a vampire was the instigator.

A few minutes passed while she went north. From below, in a hodgepodge of male and female voices, which she guessed spanned a large area, some two or three kilometers square: *I'm going to die.*

Teeth.

He's coming.

Skin.

Those eyes.

No, not my mother!

AHHHHH!

It hurts.

Never seen nails like that before.

He's so ugly.

I thought she was pretty, but this—

I'm dead.

Dead.

DEAD.

Cassie began her search over those that were face-to-face with the undead, her hope being that one of the vampires turned out to be Zach. She also listened for his name, and the sound of his own voice as he created his own thoughts and ideas.

The first seven scenes didn't involve him but other undead, only two of which she recognized.

She searched the memories of each vampire she passed over, her mind flooded with images taken from those they had killed, to other vampires they had been in contact with. It was like watching three hundred screens, each flipping through the channels at a rapid rate, each flash of content on the screen—to her vampire mind—lasting long enough for her to photograph each image and look it over to see if she had found what she was looking for. This skill, this ability to read multiple minds and process the information, was something Cassie owed to her mother. Mira was a queen telepath, able to sort through thoughts and sensations like one would search through a database. It was a skill acquired after much study and practice, taking years to master. Though Cassie wasn't as proficient nor as intelligent as her mother, she knew she was equipped enough to handle the job of finding Zach.

Between the word being spread throughout the vampire community, therefore thoughts and imagined images of Zach at the forefront of many of the undead's minds, coupled with Cassie's own telepathic search, it was merely a matter of time until following the breadcrumbs would lead her or Wil to their brother.

Cassie bet she would find him first. Though Wil was a strong telepath, like his father, he was more interested in quick and efficient killing methods, each second when encountering prey calculated and accounted for, each chemical reaction due to fear and adrenaline kept under watch in order to maximize the blood's potency once it

passed from human to the undead.
    The voices droned on. Cassie flew.
    Zach was out there somewhere.

"Y OU LIED TO me!" Rose made sure to include an extra layer of ice when she spoke.

"About?" Zach said.

Was he that clueless, or was he just playing dumb in the hopes of brushing this under the rug as a "misunderstanding"? *Or . . . how many lies has he told me*, she thought.

"I found something outside. Some*things*. Any idea what they might be?"

"What were you doing outside?" He stood there with his hands at his sides, almost defiantly.

"Answer the question."

"I don't know, what did you find, Rose?"

She guffawed and said, "You know full well what I found. Out there, by the dock?"

His expression betrayed him. He knew and, she guessed, probably felt the fool for doing such a poor job of trying to cover it up.

"Well?" she said.

Zach glanced at the door, as if he could see through it to the dock beyond and the bodies floating just beneath the water's surface. "I'm sorry. It was just something I had to do."

"That's not the point. Your need for blood aside, you still lied to me about this place, saying you found it empty and the people who owned it were not here."

"I just . . . I just didn't know how to tell you. I didn't know what you would think if . . ."

She raised her eyebrows. *Finish.*

"If you knew I drank those people's blood before we came here so *we* could come here."

She slowly shook her head. "I would have preferred the truth," she said sternly. "You could have said something. Besides, why this cabin out of all the other ones along the lake? Surely not every one of them is occupied."

"No, you're right. Others were empty. Others weren't. This one—the need I had—Rose, I was so thirsty from our time in the cave. I lost control. Honestly, I couldn't help myself. I *needed* to feed. Whatever this thing is inside me, this darkness, it completely took over. It was like I was watching myself bite into them and—"

"Save it. I don't want a play-by-play on how you end people's lives."

"It's not like that. Well, it is, but it's the way I am now. How's that different than humans killing livestock or chickens or whatever for food?"

Rose couldn't believe she was hearing this. "How is that different? How do you think?"

He was silent. "They're alive too, and—"

"You don't get it, do you?" she said. "Look at you, trying to justify murder. I might be a slayer—"

"A slayer who kills vampires."

"—a slayer who *saves* lives."

"Who kills vampires."

"Do you hear what you're saying? You didn't even answer the original question: why did you lie to me?"

"I told you."

"You told me your reasoning, but not *why*. We're not supposed to lie to each other, Zach, especially right now when we have no place to go and no one to turn to *but* each other. We need each other and you want to wreck that by sowing seeds of dishonesty between us?" She wished she could just grab his head and shake it, stir something up within that would get him to objectively think. Was his ability to rationalize his actions muted or even gone? Was he all instinct now, the survival of himself and his species the driving factor in his decision making?

"I don't know what to say."

"You don't have to say anything," she said. "I'm just really pissed at you right now. It's one thing if you lie to others. Another if it's to me."

"As if you've never lied to me before."

"That's not fair."

"Isn't it? You can point fingers at me and then expect yourself to get off scot free?"

He had her there.

The air hung thick with tension, wound so tight that Rose thought the next words out of her mouth would shatter the very fabric of existence between them and it would all come crashing down.

"I need some time alone," she said.

"What do you mean?"

"I mean—"

There was a knock at the door.

"Oh no," she said, heart suddenly hitting the gas and revving up to 2000rpms.

Zach raised a hand. "Wait." He eyed the door then went over to it.

"What are you doing?" Rose whispered as loud as she could.

Zach's hand was on the doorknob.

"Zach!"

He opened the door.

Cassie and Wil stepped into the cabin.

◆ ◆ ◆

Zach was surprised at seeing his brother and sister. He was sure that if his heart could beat, it'd be hammering in his chest faster than a bat flaps its wings.

Wil and Cassie's eyes didn't go to him first, but instead settled on Rose.

"Why did you run, Zach?" Wil asked.

"You know why," he said. *And don't even think of searching my mind for answers right now.*

"You don't have to be so hostile."

"I'm not. I'm just letting you know that I'm fine, Rose is fine, everything is fine."

"Are you sure?" Cassie said.

Zach furrowed his brow, then noticed the tears glazing over Rose's eyes. He put the thought in her brain: *What's wrong? Think your answer and I'll hear you.*

"And they'll hear us," Rose said, nodding in the direction of Cassie and Wil.

"You can't hide out here forever," Cassie said.

"We won't. This is only temporary," he said.

"And where will you go? Mother has already alerted the local covens you are wanted back home. It was how we found you. No other coven will take you in, knowing they'll have to answer to her."

"She's not their boss."

"But she's a person of influence."

Zach looked to the floor.

"She didn't tell you, did she?"

He shook his head. Wil looked at him and his expression was sympathetic.

"Mother is on the Council of Night and answers to the High Father of our kind. Her role is known to all but never spoken of unless out of necessity which, it seems, is of necessity right now."

Zach wasn't sure what to make of it, but it also made sense Mira was not all that she portrayed. The woman was cold, calculating and very skilled at the gifts of the undead. "Then just go home and tell her you didn't find me."

"I cannot lie to her," she said.

He glanced at Rose. She seemed to simply be listening with interest, however there was a busyness to her gaze that suggested she was trying to work something out within.

"Why?" Zach asked.

"Because she will read my mind and know if I am telling the truth."

"Just block her, then."

"I am nowhere nearly as skilled as she is. I've tried, believe me. She could even make you *think* you were able to stop her from intruding when in reality you haven't."

So maybe I didn't stop her from reading my mind that night in the crypt?

"She's dangerous in that way, Zach," Wil said. "You have to trust us that we know what's best for you and, now, know what's best for Rose as well."

"Leave her out of this," he said.

"There is no 'this,' Brother. There is what Mother wants and nothing else."

"And Father?"

Cassie stepped in. "He is so captivated by her that he will do anything she says even if he disagrees. My personal suspicion is she found a way to control him somehow, use his experience and strength for her own end."

"You talk about her as if she's the head of some kind

of plan or operation or something," Zach said. "Is she?"

"A place on the Council is one of the highest honors a vampire can receive," Wil said. "I'm sure she is privy to information that only a scant few know. Even her power might not be what we think it is."

This is too much, Zach thought. "Please, guys, please go. Let Rose and I stay here. We'll come out when we're ready and I'll go home."

"Home?" Rose asked, clearly curious if he was serious.

He gave her a knowing look, one he hoped would convey they wouldn't actually go but that right now she needed to trust him. "Home," he said firmly.

She turned her head, disappointed.

"We have to take you back," Cassie said. "It's either us or Mother sends in others. She's shown mercy by letting us be the ones to come get you despite the undead population being notified of your disappearance."

"What's going to happen when I go back?" Zach asked.

"We don't know."

"She didn't say anything?"

"No."

"Not very helpful," Rose said.

Wil stepped close to him, leaned in and whispered, "We can't linger here all night. The longer you wait, the worse it will get. Please, just come home."

His voice low as well, Zach said, "It's not that I want to run away, it's because of her." He meant Rose. "I love her, Wil."

"You can't. You're dead."

"It's different. I didn't just meet her. I knew her before I was reborn. All that was within me, that I lost during the change . . . it's back. The more time I spend with her, the more my old self surfaces. I can remember so much of my previous life now."

"And you'll remember more as time goes on until you've remembered it all."

"She's made me remember so quickly."

"If so, then" —Wil scanned him— "yes, this is true."

"See? Please, let me stay."

Wil seemed to consider his plea then shook his head. "I can't, I'm sorry." He stepped back beside Cassie. "Home, Zach, now."

His brother and sister's eyes met his. Time for talking was over. If he went with them now, then everything Rose and him had built until this point ran the chance of being undone. After everything they've been through, after finding each other even after death, to lose that . . .

"I'm sorry," Zach said. "I can't go."

Wil's face went firm. "Very well." In a blur of motion and wind, he left Cassie's side, then the two vampires were out the door.

"They're gone," Zach said. "I'm sorry, Rose, I didn't mean for—" He turned to where she had been standing beside him. She wasn't there.

He reached out with his mind, scanning the cabin for her presence.

There was none.

9

Rose woke up coughing, her lungs gasping for breath. It was dark all around her, the thick smell of rot and dust invading her nostrils.

"Zach?" she called. She took in another noseful of the stink and realized exactly where she was.

A coffin.

She adjusted her arms in the small space so her elbows were bent and her palms were flush against the inside of the coffin's lid. With all she had, she tried to open the wooden lid only for it to slightly budge but nothing more.

"Come on, try again," she whispered, and grunted when she pressed against the lid as hard as she could, even so far as pressing until her arms gave out from the fatigue.

It's at least a hundred pounds, she thought, *probably more.*

She banged the side of her fist against the lid's interior. "Hey! Let me out! Zach! Help!"

Coughing, she cleared her throat of the foul, dusty air. Her heart set into panic mode and tears pricked the corners of her eyes. Her father hadn't trained her for this: being trapped with the knowledge of the inevitable confrontation with the undead.

Please let it be just one. But she knew it wouldn't be like that. There'd be more.

And they'd be friends. She felt her neck with her fingertips, checking for bites. There were none. She took another moment and checked for any sensation of a bite elsewhere on her body. She was fine.

Mira, if you can hear me, please let me out and let us talk this over.

The stone lid beyond the wooden one scraped across the coffin's rim, then the wooden ones flipped open. Rose immediately sat up and coughed up more dust.

Mira stood beside her. "You called?" she said, her voice smooth, monotone.

Not funny.

"Never intended it to be."

"Stop it!"

The vampire's face remained flat.

"Why are you doing this? Why did you put me in there?"

When Mira spoke, her voice was soft, like a soothing mother. "To keep you safe. You had fallen unconscious when Wil brought you, the speed of his flight slamming the air into your lungs faster than you can manage. He should have known better, or at least kept you protected so it didn't happen, and for that we're truly sorry."

"We're?"

Wil and Cassie appeared from the shadows and came up next to her. Rose shot Wil a hot scowl. It didn't seem to faze him.

I hope Zach comes, she caught herself thinking.

"I'm sure he will," Cassie said.

"Get out of my head!"

Rain appeared beside Mira and put his arm around her. "Let this be quick," he said.

Rose's stomach dropped into her pelvis. "Make *what* quick?"

"Our time with you," Mira said.

"I don't understand."

The woman put her hand on Rose's arm. She tried to

pull it away but Mira clung tight. "Tell us what you know about the slayers. Tell us everything."

◆ ◆ ◆

As Zach flew through the air, racing back to Eagle Park Cemetery as fast as he could, he cursed himself for letting his brother and sister take Rose so easily.

I should have been ready, should have been prepared. He hoped she was all right. If his family had done anything to her—he didn't know what he'd do. Kill them? Hurt them? Or let it be?

They're using her to get me back there, he thought. *No,* he suddenly realized. *They wanted* her. *She's their link to the slayers. They were using me to get to her.*

It made perfect sense now. The way Cassie and Wil acted when they came for him, the words they spoke of Mira and her place on the Council. The fear in their eyes when they spoke of her. It was as if their lives would be forfeit if they disobeyed. Whether they were mere pawns to their mother or not, they had still given in and thus were responsible. All that time of kindness, of training, of Mira holding his hand as he found his footing in his new life as an undead—was it all a ruse? Some way to lull him into a false sense of security to build his family loyalty so strongly that, at her discretion, she would use him to bring Rose to them?

Except Mira didn't count on him falling in love. Even *he* didn't count on that. Who could? Love came as it pleased, captured him and took him away.

The night sky around him grew even darker, Rose's face fixed prominently in his mind's eye. A sharp pain rose in his chest and he immediately stopped his flight and put his hand to his breast. Hovering in the air, he tried to massage the pain away. Then he stopped, thinking that whatever just hurt him would go away in a moment as his regenerative ability kicked in and healed him.

Except the pain hung there in his chest, hollow and aching. Every thought of Rose made the pain even sharper until he winced from the discomfort.

He wasn't supposed to feel. He was a vampire, dead to the world and dead to emotion. His old life, however, came into focus and, he figured, the return of his memories had now completed their journey.

It was because of Rose, he figured, that he could feel. She was his link to his life beyond the turning and, it seemed, that old life and this new one birthed in blood and death had merged.

The pain hurt so badly he screamed at the sky, calling out Rose's name and growling at her absence and the possibility of her being in danger. The darkness within grew to prominence and rimmed his vision. Fangs burst forth in his mouth, so quickly he wasn't ready and they pierced his lower lip. He ripped his teeth from his flesh and let himself heal while the muscles and bone in his face transformed him into his true form. Nails now long with thick claws, he scraped at the air, envisioning the pain in his heart before him as he tried to tear it away.

With a shriek, he burst forward in flight and sped through the air, everything now coated in a veil of red. Soon, Eagle Park would be on the horizon. Soon, he would find Rose and destroy anyone who tried to stop him.

RAIN HELD ROSE'S hand. She was still sitting in the coffin, the vampire family surrounding her. There would be no way to escape.

"Please, calm down," Rain said. "We won't hurt you."

"How do I know that?" Rose said. "You've kidnapped me!"

"We brought you here to help us," Mira said.

Rose scowled. "No, you brought me here to pick my brain against my will."

"Please, just listen," Cassie said, placing a hand on Rose's shoulder, obviously trying to get all girl-to-girl with her.

"Don't touch me!"

"We have two options," Mira said. "You either tell us what we want to know willingly, or I go into your mind to get the information I'm looking for."

"Try it," Rose muttered.

"What was that?"

"I said try it." *Dad prepared me for this, taught me how to divide my focus so I could block the undead's intrusion into my head if I had to.*

"You must think he did a pretty good job if you're ready for me to come in there and poke around," Mira said. "Yet you haven't resisted us reading your thoughts until now."

She didn't have a reply to that. She was still new at all this and hadn't yet actually attempted to block her mind from the undead. She merely had the knowledge and some practice via mental exercises her father put her through. It might take more work than expected, now that she thought about it.

"I'm not chatting anymore," Mira said.

Rain squeezed her hand, firm enough to cement he could crush her fingers anytime he felt like it. "How many slayers are in the city?"

She kept her mouth shut and immediately focused on the fluffy, caramel-colored teddy bear that sat in the corner of her bed, up against the pillow.

"Teddy can't help you." He gave her fingers a squeeze. She flinched, but the discomfort was bearable. "How many slayers are in the city?"

Teddy's eyes were big and brown; the gloss coating applied at the factory still hadn't faded and if her bedroom light caught them just right, they sparkled at her as if winking.

"There must be many, and you must be in touch with them. I already know they work as units and teams, yet are all part of a whole, both locally and abroad. I've heard there were well over a hundred just on this side of the river alone."

Rose tuned him out. She had had Teddy for fourteen years, given to her by her mother. What the occasion was or the reason, she couldn't remember and when she had asked her mother about it, she couldn't recall either. It didn't matter though. He was soft, cute, and terribly cuddly.

"Teams of two, teams of four," Rain said. "We've encountered many. I estimated there are around two thousand slayers in this country give or take."

The black thread that made up Teddy's mouth was stitched in such a way that it wasn't a U-shaped smile, but a subtle smirk, one that said no matter how bad life got, he was always there to comfort her and make her smile again.

"STOP IT!" He squeezed her hand so hard her knuckles cracked and sharp pain burst through her fingers.

Teddy had feet that were slightly out of proportion with his legs. Big, fluffy paws that could have very well belonged to a full-grown bear instead of a stuffed one. These paws were good for hugs when no one else was around for one.

Rain's voice spiked through her mind; Teddy's adorable face vanished in a puff of black smoke. *HOW MANY ARE THERE!*

Closing her eyes, Rose brought Teddy back into view. Cold fingers grabbed her face from behind and pulled open her eyelids. She thrashed about, trying to tug away, but the fingers locked down around her head like a bear trap. She suspected they were Wil's, but couldn't be sure. Both him and Cassie were now out of view. So was Mira. Only Rain was in her left peripheral.

The shadowed stone walls of the crypt were in front of her, as well as an ornately-decorated stone coffin. She couldn't remember who it belonged to.

Stop. Focus, she told herself. *Teddy. Bring back Teddy.*

The bear's fluffy caramel face materialized before her like an apparition against the crypt's stone wall.

Rain squeezed her hand and thick, throbbing pain lashed through her index finger as he broke it. She squealed in pain and tears trickled from her eyes.

"I can break the remaining four, if you'd like," he said. "Or you can just answer the question."

Gritting her teeth, Rose focused even harder on Teddy's face, his caramel-colored fur coming back into focus.

Rain broke another finger.

♦ ♦ ♦

When Zach touched down a solid distance away from the family crypt in Eagle Park Cemetery, he immediately got to work reaching out with his mind to verify this was indeed where his family had taken Rose. His thoughts searched amongst the gravestones, past mausoleums to where his family crypt lay by the trees, underground. From this distance, the most he got were *impressions* rather than clear thoughts, but he did recognize one of those impressions belonging to Cassie. There were two other impressions. One was missing and, he suspected, it belonged to his mother.

What is she up to? he wondered and quickly ran to the mausoleum at ultra speed. Standing outside the heavy iron door, he scanned the soundwaves for voices.

From below: sobbing. Female.

Rose!

He ground his molars together, the tips of his fangs digging into the corners of his lips.

Zach raised his foot to kick down the door, but he stopped himself and turned away from the mausoleum, separating himself from the action even further. If his mother had taught him anything, it was to be patient, learn, be prepared.

But if they tried to hurt Rose, he would stop them.

♦ ♦ ♦

Teddy was dying, flickering in and out of view against the crypt's stone walls. Shivers danced up and down Rose's spine as she felt Rain pry away her control over her thoughts.

She switched her head to music, and focused on the

tune and on the lyrics.

Forty days to see the sun
Forty nights with you
Forty weeks since we've been one
And I wait
Wait
Wait

Another finger snapped. Rose bit her bottom lip and held in reaction to the pain.

Some days we win
Some days we lose
Some days I'm alone
And you carry me through

Rain let go of her hand. "I see the secrets you hold," he said, though she hoped he was just bluffing. She hadn't heard him inside her head nor felt intruded in any way, not like when they read her mind before.

Forty days under the gun
Forty nights alone
Forty weeks since it begun
When you made me wait
Wait
Wait

Her eyes burned from not blinking, the cold fingers clamped onto her head digging their tips into her skull even more.

"Show me," Rain said. "Ah, there it is."

No! He's lying. I'm not thinking about—A quick mental flash of the Slayer House manifested in her mind. She pushed it away: *Some days we win; Some days we lose; Some days I'm alone; And you carry me through.*

Wil came round to the foot of the coffin. Cassie came up behind him a moment after.

Rain took her hand again and slammed it down on

the coffin's edge, her broken fingers screaming from the impact. She howled, raw and thick with tears. The vampire's hand transformed before her, his fingers producing long, black claws half as long as the fingers themselves. He held her hand firm against the coffin's edge with one hand, and with the claw of the index finger of the other, he slowly began to burrow it into the top of her hand, blood bubbling out from the wound like oil from the ground.

And you carry me through.

Shaking, Rose held back a scream, but when Rain pushed his claw into her hand even further, she shrieked.

"Please . . ." she whispered through the pool of tears that had run down and formed on her lips. "Please stop."

"Tell us what we want to know without resisting and I'll stop." Rain shoved his claw in even more to cement his point. Rose feared he'd break through clear to the other side of her hand if he pushed any harder.

Muscles in her hand and wrist locking, their spasms sending a shockwave of pain through her forearm and up to her shoulder, she softly said, "And you carry me through."

The fingers on her head increased their pressure and black and green rimmed her vision; a low buzzing grew in her ears.

From the side, the voice hollow and distant: "Let me handle this." It was Mira. She smoothly walked up to the foot of the coffin and stood in front of her children. In a blur, Wil and Cassie suddenly appeared on the other side of the coffin opposite their father.

Mira's eyes met Rose's then moved up to the one who held her head in their grasp. The pressure on her skull increased and all went black, ears ringing.

The back and top of her head aching, Rose woke up on her back in the coffin, her father looking down on her.

ROSE'S CRIES FROM below the crypt pierced Zach's ears and his heart. Furious, he put his hands to the iron door and pushed inward with all he had. The hinges popped off their sockets and the heavy door slammed down onto the stone floor of the mausoleum. He quickly strode through to the next door and kicked it off its frame. The door tumbled down the stone steps in a series of solid booms. Nothing but rage consuming him, he leaped down to the bottom of the steps and entered the crypt proper where his family stood around Mira's coffin, Rose lying within. A vampire that loomed over his love at the head of the coffin was already changing to its disfigured form before Zach could get a clear look at its face.

"Let her go!" he said.

Rose's faint voice met his ears. "Zach . . ."

"Nice of you to join us, son," Mira said.

With a growl, Zach jumped into the air, arms outstretched, ready to jump on her and tear her apart. Mira disappeared before he could and he crashed into the base of the coffin, rocking it. His mother stood at his feet.

"Is that any way to treat your mother?" she asked.

A strong pair of hands picked him up from behind and tossed him aside. He skidded across the floor and into the base of his own coffin. He got to his feet and made another charge, this time at Rain. His father's feet left the ground and met him midair, the two colliding in a tangle and dropping to the stone floor. Rain bore his fangs, hissing. With a hard right hook, Zach punched him in the side of his skeletal head, then came back with his left hand, fingers splayed, tearing a piece out of his father's face. Rain growled; the skin and tissue upon his face reformed and healed.

His father raised his own set of claws and rammed them deep into Zach's gut.

"Father, no!" Cassie yelped from the other side of the room.

"Quiet," Mira said, her tone firm.

Rain brought his face close to Zach's and twisted his hand against his son's stomach, causing the claws biting into his flesh to grip even tighter. Fighting back the pain, Zach spat blood on his father's face.

Rain didn't flinch. "Son, I understood what you're going through. I really did. But coming in tonight like you had is unacceptable." He twisted his claws. "You will never usurp your mother's or my authority again, understand?"

Zach growled.

The claws tearing into him drew closer together, ripping his guts even further. "Understand!"

Without a word, Zach brought his arm around and used the claws of the index fingers of both hands to stab his father in the eyes. Once they were plunged in the eye sockets, he yanked them out, taking Rain's eyeballs with them.

Screeching, Rain leaped back and crouched on the floor, cradling his face. It was only temporary, Zach knew, but he would take whatever advantage he could get to see Rose to safety.

His poor girl still lay in the coffin, the unfamiliar vampire standing at her head holding her down by the shoulders, his grasp firm despite her thrashing about.

Screaming, she let out wet gasps filled with fear and tears. He noticed the creature wore the same coat that Mira had darned the other night, the one that belonged to his father even though the vampire now wearing it was someone else.

Wasting no time, Zach hurled himself at the creature, nailing him in the shoulder with his own, the two slamming up against the stone wall at the opposite end. Before he could deliver a blow to the creature, Wil grabbed him from behind and pulled him away.

"That's enough," Wil shouted. He bore his fangs.

"Never," Zach said through gritted teeth. *Not when it comes to Rose.* His midsection was already on the mend, but it still hurt with fiery pain.

"She's the enemy. She's a slayer. You can't side with her."

"I will!" The words were out and never felt more right.

Wil bit into his shoulder, producing a sheet of blood that spurt upward then splashed down on Zach's skin and ran down his body.

Letting the darkness within him overtake the moment, Zach bore the pain, ripped his arm and shoulder free from his brother's mouth, and pressed his clawed fingers together to form a spear, and drove the claws home into his brother's heart.

All the commotion in the room went still as Wil looked at him wide-eyed, his lips slightly pursed as if about to ask, "Why?" His brother's body grew heavy against his claws, but he did not let go. Bone slid beneath flesh as Wil's visage returned to his human form before he exploded in a puff of ash.

Mira howled like a banshee, her smooth skin now filled with craters and wrinkles as it stretched across a misshaped head and a mouth bearing razor sharp fangs. She spun through the air like a corkscrew. Zach sped to the side to avoid her. Once on the other side of the room, Rain grabbed him, kicked him in the legs from behind, folding his weight under him as Mira appeared beside him.

Beyond his parents, the unfamiliar vampire pushed Rose back into the coffin as she attempted to climb over the edge.

Cassie joined her mother's side.

A thick forearm slipped under Zach's neck, pulled, while another hand took his arm and bent it behind his back like a chicken wing.

Mira merely eyed him, her gaudy face and permanent scowl slowly checking Zach over as if looking for something. She pulled away and said, "You didn't tell her."

He didn't know what she meant.

Rain tugged back with his forearm, tightening his grip.

"Tell her," Mira said.

"Tell her what?"

With a mere glance, Mira told the creature holding down Rose to hoist the girl up and make her face him. The vampire obeyed and set her upright, her legs dangling over the edge of the elevated coffin.

"Say it," his mother hissed.

I don't know what you want me to say, he told her.

Mira spoke into his mind: *Tell her you killed her mother.*

"No."

The muscles in his neck began to compress as his father squeezed even harder.

"Either you tell her or I will," Mira said.

It was evident by Cassie's confused expression she

didn't know what was going on. "Tell her what? What happened?"

Without her eyes leaving Zach's, Mira said, "Your brother has something to say to his beloved. Something important."

Across the room, Rose looked at him, eyes already softening like they did when she wanted him to tell the truth.

"I . . . I can't," he said.

"Tell her, Zach, whatever it is," Cassie said. "It's the least you could do after what you did to Wil."

He closed his eyes and thought back to the night of his first feed, and the way Mira had made him feel special, as if he was accomplishing something great. It was that night that started all this, the memories gained from Shelly Jordan alerting him to his previous life, Rose, and his connection to her and her family. If he hadn't fed upon her, then perhaps tonight could have been avoided. Perhaps Rose could have been safe and could have never seen the ugliness of this existence.

When he opened his eyes, he said, "I'm so sorry. I didn't know. I didn't mean to."

Clearly enjoying this, Mira drew in beside him and said in his ear loud enough for Rose to hear: "Didn't mean to do *what?*"

The weight on the air was so thick one could swim through it.

Rose was confused; he didn't need to read her mind to tell. He knew her too well.

Just say it. If you love her, you'll tell her, even if you lose her in the end. "Rose, I . . . I killed your mother."

His love's shoulders sunk as the shock hit her. She didn't say anything and merely dropped her eyes to her feet. When she spoke, the words barely formed.

"You did?"

Heart breaking, Zach said, "Please, I didn't know. Mother took me out to teach me how to hunt. Your mom had been captured. I didn't know it was her, I swear. My memory wasn't . . . . Please. Please. I'm sorry. So sorry!"

She began to tremble, so much so she fell into the arms of the creature that kept her sitting. The creature caught her and merely held her.

A sadistic grin spread across Mira's face. "Ah, and now it has ended. You have hurt us, son, and now we have hurt you."

Speechless, he hung his head, unable to believe what he just told the love of his life, the love of his rebirth.

If I could take it back, Rose, I swear I would. Please forgive me, he thought.

The pain in his heart swelled until it felt like someone was stabbing him in the chest. Darkness grew around his vision as his pain turned to hate. A low hiss built in his throat and came out of his mouth, the only way to expel the pain. Except—

Zach tucked his chin in and pushed his head back against his father's hold so that he was able to get his chin part way in between where Rain's forearm met his neck. He bit down as hard as he could, shaking his head as he did so, tearing the flesh from his father's arm. Rain let go; Zach dropped to the floor, his mouth full of dead meat. His father's blood was thick and syrupy, the funk of its decay making it to the back of his throat and into his nose. Zach wondered if he'd gain any of his father's memories after tasting his blood. But where he did or not he had to get Rose out of here. Now it was purely about survival and nothing else, purely about a future with the girl he loved if she ever found it in her heart to forgive him. With as much speed as he could muster, he zipped around his mother, slashed out at the creature that held Rose in the coffin, then picked up his love and sped her up the stairs and out the door.

They were in the sky immediately upon exit. He slowed down so Rose could manage easier.

She gripped him tight as he held her in his arms and started to cry.

12

THE EMPTY AIR beneath Rose's feet seemed to grab at her ankles, the gravity of seeing her father transformed into one of the undead coupled with Zach's new family trying to kill them both wanting to pull her down to the ground and make her plummet to her death.

"Hold on," Zach said firmly, and quickly tightened his grip around her and bent them both one hundred and eighty degrees so they pointed straight down to the cemetery below.

Wind rushed by Rose's cheeks as they descended, gravity collecting blood in her head and making it feel full. Zach cranked on the speed, his face chiseled from stone, nothing but determination in his eyes. Though he was disfigured while in his undead form, the way he cared for her was beautiful.

With a twist of their bodies, Zach brought them horizontal to the ground and zipped through the treetops. Rose glanced past their feet; Rain was hot on their tail, his teeth bared, his face a skeletal monster of stretched skin over well-muscled flesh.

"I'm going to roll you," Zach told her. "Roll to the left as fast as you can the second I let go."

"What? You're going to drop me?"

"Not exactly. I've blocked my father from entering my mind, but he is more skilled than I and will break through any moment. Be strong. I'll come for you. Ready?"

"No!" Her heart galloped.

"Left side, Rose, left side."

Zach dipped lower and the ground rushed up to meet her. "Nothing is more important than your safety," he whispered, and in that moment, she believed him.

Left, left, left, she told herself.

The gray, moon-lit grass was right beneath her.

Without a word, Zach dropped her, and she rolled left, the sky and grass exchanging places as she tumbled along the ground, body prone, as if rolling down a hill but without the decline. Every second she rolled felt like a minute, and her stomach danced inside her as it violently sloshed the little contents it had.

Finally, her roll began to slow; two more rolls and she came to a stop on her face, the ground beneath her body and outstretched arms seeming to tilt up and right and down and left over and over again, like lying on an unbalanced table.

Head swimming, dizziness rocking her brain, she tried to push herself up; her arms gave out beneath her when her hand and fingers cried out in pain. Her face smacked up against the ground, her nose exploding in a hard electric tingle that she felt all the way into her forehead and the inside corners of her eyes.

Lying there, catching her breath, she closed her eyes and gathered herself to try and get up again.

A pair of hands grabbed her from behind and yanked her to her feet. The moment her heels touched the ground, the grass beneath her wobbled like a teeter-totter.

Cassie stood before her, claws drawn, mouth open, fangs out.

◆ ◆ ◆

Ascending as high as he could, Zach climbed through

the sky, passing the clouds, and wondered how much higher he had to go before he'd escape Earth's atmosphere and wind up in space.

A pair of clawed hands with a steel-like grip caught hold of his ankles and jerked him down before hurling him to the earth. Zach somersaulted through the air before what felt like a freight train cut in from the side, took hold of him, and drove him down even further.

"You don't need to do this!" Zach said. "Please, Father, stop!"

Rain merely hissed and opened his mouth wide, his fangs seeming longer than when Zach last saw them.

Wind whistled and rushed by at such speed that if Zach didn't free himself, his father would plow them into the ground and kill them both. Curling his fingers, Zach reached out and tore at Rain's middle, slashing his guts open and letting the intestines within hang out and flap on the breeze like a series of torn flags. His hyper-sensitive hearing heard the moist squish of flesh knitting into flesh as his father's body repaired itself.

With a quick shot to the face, he momentarily distracted Rain, enough for his father's grip to temporarily loosen. Zach swung out again, this time bringing his claws across his father's face and neck, hoping to sever the head at the throat. Blood gushed out on impact, spraying them both, but unfortunately his claws only made it about halfway through and didn't cut the head off entirely.

The ground was getting closer. Zach tried again, this time the plan to slash with one set of claws at the front of the neck, the other to tear open the back and hopefully meet in the middle. It might not kill his father, but it might be enough to slow him down so he could get to Rain's heart and tear it out. Right now his own legs were up against his father's chest and there wasn't enough leverage to penetrate the heart.

Summoning all his strength, Zach readied his hands and in one swift motion managed to tear open the back of his father's neck, but Rain twisted his head when the first set of claws came through, in turn forcing the other set to slice his jaw open instead of the front of his throat.

Shadowed treetops came up below.

He realized what his father was going to do.

Zach smiled at the idea, and he got ready to fly. As the treetops neared, Zach searched his own mind to ensure his father's presence was absent. Not sensing him, he got ready and when the trees were a mere fifteen or twenty feet away, he hugged his father by the shoulders and wrapped his legs around Rain's middle, latching onto him like a crab. With a mighty twist, Zach spun them around so he was on top. In a blur, he released his legs but kept his arms steady. Rain's back hit the trees; the branches snapped in loud, echoing pops as they plummeted through.

Zach tipped his body so he did a handstand on top of his father and drove Rain down on a series of branches, the hard wood ripping through his father's body like a bed of spikes. Blood and flesh splattered against Zach's face and chest. He didn't care. His father had hurt Rose, had caused her pain, had aided in condemning him to this existence.

They struck the ground; Zach rolled off him, the impact of hitting the ground with such force breaking his hands. Wild pain shot through his hands and arms.

Screaming, he tumbled to the side of his father's limp form. The moment he stopped rolling along the ground, he sprang to his feet and ran to Rain as his hands healed and bones realigned themselves, muscle and ligaments stitching themselves back together.

Rain lay on the ground, over a half dozen branches sticking out from his chest and through his thighs. One looked like it had struck his heart, and though his father lie there, his face and hands already back to their human form, Zach tore one of the branches free from Rain's body and rammed it directly into his heart, just in case.

A wild shriek to his right tore him from the moment. *Rose!*

◆ ◆ ◆

"We were supposed to be sisters!" Cassie screeched into Rose's ear while she lay on top of her, pinning her to the ground.

Rose cried out and wrestled against the young vampire's immense strength. It was no use. Cassie had her pinned.

"Wil's dead because of you!" the vampire screeched.

She's acting like she actually cares, like she actually has feelings, Rose thought. Then again, Zach had feelings, or so portrayed himself as if he did. Her father had taught her that vampires were devoid of emotion since their bodies no longer produced the chemicals and hormones required for emotion and attachment. It was one of the reasons why they were such good killers. *Was he wrong?*

"Not because of me—" she started but Cassie slapped her in the face, her claws dragging across her flesh on the follow-through, cutting her open. Rose's face stung; warm blood ran down her cheek and pooled in her ear and tickled her neck.

Her hand throbbed and she couldn't move her broken fingers. She desperately wished she had on her body armor, wished she had her weapons. Now, defenseless, there was no way out from underneath Cassie. The only tool she had was her mouth. Maybe if she could keep Cassie talking, maybe it would buy Zach enough time to find her and rescue her. She was confident he wouldn't leave her completely alone in the cemetery with the undead family.

"Cassie, please," Rose said, "you have to let me go. I *love* your brother."

The vampire grimaced and a low growl rumbled in the back of its throat.

"And he loves me," she continued.

"He can't love you," Cassie hissed. "He cannot feel anything."

She was getting tired of hearing that. "But he can," she said, tears wetting her eyes at the thought of how much Zach did love her, how he fought back from death just for her. "He does. He remembers everything."

"Memory or not, it isn't possible. Zach is no longer human."

"Maybe not, but I *know* him. Know him better than you or anyone. The way he is with me, it's the Zach I knew and the boy who loves me." Softly, she added, "Please don't kill me. What will you tell him? How will he react?"

Cassie seemed to weigh her words, then the veiny muscles around her eyes drew taught. "I'm going to bleed you dry, then I'm going to wear your carcass as a coat."

Rose bit down, grinding her teeth together, bracing herself for the set of fangs to pierce her. She experienced similar pain before, as part of her training, when her father punctured her arm with a fossilized set of jaguar teeth. Every muscle had locked when the fangs bit into her arm, the surrounding area of the wound quickly growing numb. She hardly felt the blood running down her arm until her dad pulled the teeth out.

She could only imagine what that would feel like on her neck when Cassie bit in.

"Before you bite," Rose said, "I just want to say: tell Zach I love him."

Cassie grinned. "I won't," and moved in for the kill. Her face suddenly locked with mouth wide open as something struck her in the back. Soon, Cassie's body was lifted from on top of Rose, revealing Marcus with his claws dug deep into Cassie's back. He tossed the vampire's body aside, growling.

Body shaking with adrenaline, Rose got to her feet and ran as fast as she could on rubbery legs.

13

MIRA HAD SWOOPED in before Zach could make his way to Rose and save her. It seemed every strike he was about to make, Mira countered with ease, even so far as *playing* with him instead of actually fighting.

"Mother, I'm your son," Zach said. "Let us start over."

"You killed your father and your brother. You betrayed your brethren. You will die for your treason."

"You were so kind to me," he said.

"Only to make you believe you were important. The truth is: no one is important. Especially not you."

"I'm . . . one of you."

She grinned. "No, you're not nor ever were."

But you saved me. "Mother . . ."

"I didn't save you from anything. I *stole* you."

You said . . . ". . . you brought me back home, to the crypt, made me a vampire like I was supposed to be. Do you mean—"

"I lied."

Can't be.

"You're human, Zach. Nothing more other than your blood contains ours. You were our link to Rose, carefully selected so as to play the part in bringing her to us so we could—" She rolled her index fingers one on top of the other, encouraging him to finish.

"Use her to infiltrate the slayers."

"Just a pawn. I don't love you, Zach." Her eyes met his and—

All went white. When his vision cleared, he was at home, with his human parents, seated at the dinner table. His dad sat at the head of it, his mother opposite. Zach sat to his dad's right, his brother across from him.

"Where did—" he started, wanting to know where Mira went and how he suddenly got here with his old family.

He tried to get up, but couldn't, his ankles bound to the chair legs with rough rope, his wrists tied as well, the other end of the rope connected to the top of the chair legs just below the seat. He could only raise his hands as high as his stomach, not even high enough to reach the tabletop.

His parents and brother were bound as well.

Mira stood in the corner of the kitchen, near the sink. The white cabinets above the countertop that lined the far wall and right side of the kitchen were spackled with blood.

Another white flash and Zach caught sight of his dad with his head bowed, a big blotch of blood on his forehead, as if someone had cracked the front of his skull open. His mom and brother had their heads bowed, too, and though his family was breathing, they were unconscious and blood leaked from their lips and ran in long, syrupy strings to their laps.

"What did you do to—" he started but held his tongue when he noticed the table before him was covered in torn, bloody flesh, innards, a pair of eyes, teeth, a couple of them long sharp fangs.

"This is what happened to Cassie," Mira said. "Take a good look because this is what I will now do to your family. Your *real* family."

"Please don't!" Zach snapped, then, quieter, "Please, I beg you."

"You're making it sound like you actually care for them. *Really* care."

"I do."

"Then prove it. Stop your resisting and let me have Rose. If you do, your family will be spared. If you don't, Rose will die after I extract from her all the information I need."

"Leave her out of this."

Mira came closer and leaned in toward him. "Why should I? It was because of her this all started."

"You started it."

"Still makes it because of her."

"Mira . . . Mother, please. I'll do what you say, but, please, leave Rose alone."

"You'll sacrifice your family instead?"

"I'll sacrifice neither."

"That's not a choice."

"It'll have to be."

Mira slinked in behind Zach's brother and with one swift sweep of her arm, slashed his brother's neck from the rear. She nearly cleaved through to the other side and his brother's head lolled to the left and down so far that the boy's forehead was almost touching his chest, his gray sweatshirt stained maroon with the liter of blood that gushed out.

"Okay, okay! Wait. Stop," Zach said.

Her eyes bore into his. He didn't even have to pause and search his mind to know she was in there.

"Now we're getting somewhere," she said.

"You could just kill me now, and—" He stopped short, not wanting to finish by saying, *And Rose would be yours.*

"You're right," she said, "but if you die, Rose would most certainly become a martyr. Teenagers. Puppy love.

Her ignorance would force her to give up."

"Then you'll have to start all over. You might not get the memories you need."

She simply nodded.

Casually, she walked over to where Zach's mom sat slumped in her chair. With a quick tug of his mom's hair, Mira yanked her head back. Her hands moved so quick that a second later her claw shot through clean to the other side and stuck out of his mom's forehead. A swirl of blood pooled around the base of the claw and quickly ran over his mom's temples and face.

"Stop!" he screamed. Tears wet his eyes and both him and Mira paused in disbelief.

A moment more and Mira jerked her claw out of his mom's head and let it flop to the side.

"Mom . . ." Zach said, his voice so quiet that even his acute hearing barely picked it up. Rage flooded through him and the darkness of the hunt formed around his vision anew, bathing Mira, the blood-and-flesh-coated table, and his family in a red and yellow haze.

He pulled hard against the restraints, surprised that mere rope was able to hold him. Perhaps Mira telekinetically strengthened his bonds. The rough rope worked against his skin like a saw; produced a ring of blood and torn flesh around his wrists. A second after each tear, his skin repaired itself. He didn't think he'd have time to wear his wrists and hands down so thin against the rope that he could simply slip out of it.

Wait. I cou— He silenced the thought immediately, not wanting to give Mira warning.

Ultra speed was a tremendous ally to the vampire. It enabled one to move from place to place inside of a blink, catch prey off guard, and find refuge instantly should one be discovered. Zach channeled that speed into his hands and forearms and twisted them side-to-side as fast as he could, the rope around his skin immediately digging into his flesh. Each searing slice sent a hot wave of pain through his hands and arms. The blood quickly gushing from his wrists made him briefly wonder that if he lost enough, would he actually die, or was it just human memory talking?

Mira was at his side in a blink, her hands already on his wrists to stop him.

It was too late. He was out. With a growl, he lunged toward her face first and mouth open, and clamped down on the first bit of flesh to greet his fangs. It turned out to be just above his mother's collarbone. He jerked his head back and pulled free a hunk of meat, blood spurting up from the wound. Mira shrieked.

Claws at the ready, Zach spun on his heels and moved to cut his dad loose. Mira grabbed him from behind, blood from her collarbone soaking through Zach's shirt. The smell of the blood—even *undead* blood—excited him and a surge of vigor stoked the fire for revenge. He rammed his elbows back into her gut, spun around, grabbed her from behind the head and brought her face down on his knee with all his might. Her skull split on his kneecap, the kneecap dislocating from the force of the blow. He dropped to the floor from the pain. So did she.

Dad, he thought, and scrambled to his slumped form in the chair. He severed his bonds and hoisted him over his shoulder, his run to the front room at first burdened by a limp, but as his knee healed itself, he turned on the speed full tilt.

The living room was just as he remembered it: the full sofa on his right, the love seat across from it, the room divided in two by the matching, flower-patterned comfy chair, the one his dad usually sat on Saturday mornings while reading the paper. To the left was the front landing and door. Zach ran up to it, twisted the knob and pulled. It didn't budge. He double checked the deadbolt. It was unlocked. He tried the knob again; nothing.

What?

Mira came flying out of the kitchen, screeching, heading straight for him with her claws pointed at his face. He sped out of the way; she stopped just short of the door, landed, and turned around.

Zach backed into the living room, his dad still slung over his shoulder. He gave him a quick bump to try and wake him, but it didn't work.

Mira opened her mouth, eyes wide with bloodlust and hissing like a snake. Zach backed up toward the front window. The curtains were drawn. Didn't matter. He'd fly backward and crash through the glass and take his dad to safety.

With a leap, he soared backward through the air, hit the curtains and what felt like a brick wall behind them. He landed on his knees, the shock of the impact and his dad's weight upon him locking them beneath him.

In a blur, Mira was beside him and pulled his dad away, hurling the man's unconscious form across the room. His dad hit the drywall, broke it, and fell to the carpet.

"No!" Zach shouted.

Mira grabbed him by the shirt, shook him and slammed him back against the curtained window. Like before, it didn't break but felt like smashing up against brick. The curtain rod released from above, hit Zach's head then fell to the floor. Mira delivered a quick punch to the face, spinning Zach around and facing the window. It was indeed glass, and beyond, the cemetery, Rose fifty yards away amongst a row of tombstones running away from . . . her father.

"Marcus had turned," he said. "But this . . ." *This isn't real,* he thought. "This is—"

He extended his claws, turned around, and slashed a thick line across Mira's neck. Quickly, he came back with the other hand and slashed the same spot again, severing her head from her body. The head hit the carpet by her feet, blood oozing from it. Her headless corpse folded backward nearly in half, then collapsed.

Zach readied himself because at any moment, this illusion created by Mira would fade because of her death and he'd be free to slaughter the last vampire that needed to die tonight.

The window remained. He beat against the glass with his fists, floated up into the air and kicked at it. It didn't break, not even a crack.

Behind him, he sensed Mira rising to her feet.

16

Gasping for breath, unable to run any further, her father merely lurching behind her with a wide gait, Rose stopped and turned around. Her heart ached within as her father just stared at her, unmoving, and for the briefest of moments, she thought he recognized her.

"Oh, Dad," she said. "Look what they've done to you. I thought . . . I thought you were dead." She breathed in and exhaled slowly. "And I guess you are."

Marcus merely grimaced at her, his face distorted and twisted into a bony mess of contortion underneath a thin tarp of skin.

She wondered if she should just run away. *He'd only follow me again.* There had to be a way to hide from him, to just stop and try and figure things out. She glanced up and searched the sky for Zach. Nothing was visible in between the trees.

Zach, are you there? Can you hear me? As loud as she could: "Zach?"

Marcus growled at her, sending a jolt throughout her body. To herself: "Remember your training, remember your training." She breathed out hard through pursed lips. "Focus, focus." She glanced over her shoulder. Zach was on the other end of the gravestones, just standing there, Mira behind him, her hand on his shoulder.

"Zach!" she screamed. *Zach, please!* He didn't respond, didn't move, not even when her father tackled her to the ground and the sharp sting of fangs dug into her back.

◆ ◆ ◆

"The only way you can save her now," Mira said, her head having grown and reformed on her body, the severed one not far from her feet, "is to deliver her to us. I promise to not hurt her if you do. I will get my answers and set her free. Both of you."

"I don't believe you," Zach said through gritted teeth.

"I tell you the truth."

"Didn't her father give up his memories in his turning? Why not use those?"

"Her father did give up memories, but he was also smart. He must have known the night of his turning would be his last battle, so he erased his knowledge of the Slayer Order via hypnosis prior to his arrival at the cemetery. I give him credit for that. So far as he was aware, there was no Order. Just him. A freelance slayer. Nothing more. He even hid his base of operations from us.

"Now, Like I said, bring Rose to me and you will both be spared. It's the truth, Zach."

"Just like how you made me believe I was back home with my family? Just like how you said I really belonged to you but I didn't?"

"That was different. I am telling you the truth right now."

He shook his head. "I'm going to kill you."

"You already tried and you failed. Besides, there is nothing here for you to kill me with."

Grimacing, Zach said, "Wrong." He dropped to the ground, grabbed the curtain rod, spun around and rammed the pointy stainless steel end into Mira's heart.

She teetered back a few steps, then fell over when her legs buckled beneath her. Zach calmly went and stood over her, fists clenched.

"How . . . how could you?" she said, blood already leaking from the corners of her mouth. "You're my son."

"No. You said I wasn't. You're just a vampire, like me, but one that went too far." He paused. "You thought you were going to help us survive, but instead you've only escalated the war. Instead, you've shown me the ugliness of our species, one built on lies that will eventually rob us of our power."

She coughed up another gob of blood. "You . . . you don't know what you're talking about. You can't . . . possibly . . . understand the scope of our race and our true place in this world. I was . . . was going to show you one day." Her body went limp, slumped against the curtain rod, which slid through her even further. "I'm sorry I lied. You really are my s—" Her body dissolved into a spray of flesh and ash. A flash of white sparked before Zach's vision and he was in the cemetery.

Mira's hand was on his shoulder, but was already turning to dust. By the time he turned around to face her, she was nothing more than a pile of ashes on the grass at his feet.

"She better be dead for real." *Rose!* he thought. He took off, turned around, and headed right toward Marcus. The vampire had its mouth pressed hard against Rose's back as she lay there with her face to the grass.

Zach plowed into Marcus and knocked him off her body. Not wasting any time, he slashed Marcus's hands at the wrists, cutting them clean off, jumped into the air and kicked the vampire in the head. Marcus went straight back. Zach sped to the nearest tombstone, punched at it full force; the stone split and broke into sharp, jagged pieces. He picked up the nearest one, glanced at Rose, who lay still on the grass, bleeding out from her back.

Zach landed on top of Marcus and slammed the pointed stone home into his chest, piercing his heart.

The vampire howled as death overtook him.

"I'm sorry, Mr. Jordan," Zach said. "I had no choice." He spoke into his fellow vampire's mind: *I'm so sorry. If you're able, please forgive me. I'll take good care of Rose, I promise.*

Blood poured out from Marcus's chest and in a burst of gray and pink, he turned to blood-laced ash and disintegrated beneath Zach's body.

His vampire ears listened intently for Rose's heartbeat.

He heard none.

15

BLOOD SOAKED THE grass around Rose's body in a crimson puddle. Zach's knees sloshed against the blood when he knelt down beside her.

"Oh no . . ." he said, and a sharp pain struck his heart. For a moment he thought a slayer had pierced him, but when he saw he was intact, he realized the pain was for her. A tiny beacon of life in his undead body.

Ever so gently, he turned her head on its side. "Can you hear me?"

She didn't reply. Her eyes were closed and no breath escaped her lungs.

"Don't die, no, no, please don't die. You can't. Not like this. Not this way. You can't leave me. I don't want to be alone. I don't want to be this without you. I love you. Rose!" He screamed into the night air, not caring if a hundred slayers heard his cries.

Gently, he placed his hand on her head, his fingers stroking her hair.

The smell of her blood tickled his nostrils and the darkness swelled around his vision. It came on so thick he could barely see.

No, not Rose. Not like this. She's dead, you can't drink. "So thirsty," he whispered. The night's ordeal must have drained him.

Boiled rage and unstoppable anger consumed him. Growling at the top of his lungs, grief taking over, he yearned for comfort. But there was no one to give it to him.

Blood.

Blood could make the pain go away. Could make the memory of her last forever.

But not Rose's. I can't—

The darkness quickly overwhelmed him and he gave in to the thirst, the will to fight suddenly absent, and he bit down hard on Rose's neck and began to drink her blood.

♦ ♦ ♦

Kissing Rose WAS like kissing blood: warm, smooth, sweet; a gentleness to her lips that made Zach cry out for more. When their lips met, his heart held hers and she his; her life flashed before his eyes and he knew her better than she knew herself.

As their lips playfully melded, separated, merged, he held her close, his embrace gentle and careful, yet firm enough so she knew he'd never let go. Her arms wrapped tightly around his neck, he sensed that if it was possible, she'd pull him deep into herself and make their bodies one. Instead, Rose's hands tugged behind his neck, her fingers stroking its nape, letting him know how much she loved him.

Tongues gliding across each other's, Zach was ever cautious that Rose didn't accidentally drag her tongue across his fangs and cut herself. The last thing he wanted to do was hurt her. They'd already been down the road of pain, loneliness and separation. For something to happen to set them on that path again, he couldn't bear it.

Even now, standing here with her, holding her, kissing her, there was the underlying trepidation that something might go wrong.

Zach's heart raced with phantom beats, his uneasiness

at the prospect of losing her distracting him from their kiss.

Rose must have sensed it because she pulled slightly away and said, "What's wrong?"

"I just . . . I love you so much," he whispered. "I never thought—"

She placed the soft skin of her fingertips across his lips. "Shhh." And drew her to him.

Their lips met and Zach's world exploded in flashes of Rose growing up, a little girl with brown hair in pigtails wrapped in purple ribbon all the way to the gorgeous sixteen-year-old she was now.

The images—flying photographs wrapped in light— not just mere pictures but each a snapshot of Rose's time on this earth oozing with meaning and life, their display not just impacting his mind's eye but also his heart. Though each image flashed but for an instant, the sensations crashing through him drew on, the events depicted happening in real time. A nightmare when she was three; a pizza party for her and her girlfriends when she was six; the cake falling off its tray as her mother tried to bring it to her on her tenth birthday; her first pimple; her dad giving her the keys to the car when she got her license.

It was Rose's life that kept Zach connected to the realm of the living. His life . . . he didn't know it, at least not in the way he should. These past few weeks with Rose were all he knew by way of life.

Standing here at the edge of the abyss in a realm where there was only darkness, hovering between the world of the living and the dead, him and Rose held each other and gazed off together as if overlooking a canyon of night.

"I'm sorry, sweetie, it had to come to this. It was the

only way," he said. "Your father started it. I had to finish it."

She leaned her head on his shoulder and said, "It's okay. Really, I understand."

"You do?"

"I do."

"I thought that you couldn't accept certain parts of me."

"At first I thought I could, then the enormity of it all just pulled me down."

"Understandable."

"But tonight, you changed everything for me. You went back on your own, just for me. And you made me one with you, just for me."

"I love you, Rose."

"I love you, too, Zach."

He put the knuckle of his index finger under her chin and drew her face up to his. Their lips met, fit perfectly together, and he brought her close, hoping that all he felt, all his love, would pour into her—

—and bring her back to life.

About the Author

A.P. Fuchs is the author of many novels and short stories, most of which have been published. His most recent books are *Possession of the Dead, Magic Man Plus 15 Tales of Terror* and *Zombie Fight Night: Battles of the Dead*, in which zombies fight such classic monsters as werewolves, vampires, Bigfoot, and even go up against awesome foes like pirates, ninjas, and . . . Bruce Lee.

A.P. Fuchs is also known for his superhero series, *The Axiom-man Saga*, and the author of the shoot 'em up zombie trilogy, *Undead World*. He also edited the zombie anthologies *Dead Science* and *Vicious Verses and Reanimated Rhymes: Zany Zombie Poetry for the Undead Head*.

Fuchs lives and writes in Winnipeg, Manitoba.

Visit his corner of the Web at
www.canisterx.com

Check out the *Undead World Trilogy* at
www.undeadworldtrilogy.com

And follow him on Twitter at
www.twitter.com/ap_fuchs

Did you know **A.P. Fuchs** writes love stories under the pen name **Peter Fox**?

For touching love stories that tug at the heartstrings, look no further than the following:

When a quirky girl named April suddenly sits across from Joseph Bailey at a quiet coffee shop, nothing can prepare him for the weekend ahead and how it'll change him forever.

Jack used to believe in angels.
Her name was Cyan, and they were in love.

Peter Fox books are available in paperback and eBook at Amazon.com or your favorite online retailer.

A.P. Fuchs
Zombie Collection

Axiom-man
The Dead Land
ISBN 978-1-897217-83-2

Blood of the Dead
ISBN 978-1-897217-80-1

Possession of the Dead
ISBN 978-1-926712-53-6

Vicious Verses and
Reanimated Rhymes
ISBN 978-1-897217-95-5

Available at Amazon.com, BarnesandNoble.com
or your favorite online retailer.

Also available through your favorite bookstore.

www.coscomentertainment.com

www.ingramcontent.com/pod-product-compliance
Lightning Source LLC
Chambersburg PA
CBHW031255210726

48287CB00003B/1041